Geronimo Stilton

Thea Stilton
THE JOURNEY
TO ATLANTIS

Scholastic Inc.

Library of Congress Cataloging-in-Publication data available.

ISBN 978-0-545-44020-2

Based on an original idea by Elisabetta Dami.
www.geronimostilton.com

Published by Scholastic Inc., 557 Broadway, New York, NY 10012.
SCHOLASTIC and associated logos are trademarks and/or registered trademarks of Scholastic Inc.

Stilton is the name of a famous English cheese. It is a registered trademark of the Stilton Cheese Makers' Association. For more information, go to www.stiltoncheese.com.

Text by Thea Stilton
Original title *Nel Regno di Atlantide: Il principe di Atlantide*
Cover by Danilo Barozzi
Illustrations by Barbara Pellizzari and Chiara Balleello
Color by Alessandro Muscillo
Graphics by Yuko Egusa and Marta Lorini

Special thanks to Tracey West
Translated by Julia Heim
Interior design by Kay Petronio

12 11 10 9 8 7 6 5 4 3 2 1   12 13 14 15 16 17/0

Printed in Singapore   46
First printing, October 2012

Hi, I'm Thea Stilton, Geronimo Stilton's sister! I am a special correspondent for The Rodent's Gazette, the most famouse newspaper on Mouse Island. I also teach adventure journalism at Mouseford Academy. The story I'm about to tell you features the Thea Sisters—five really special students. They love adventure as much as I do! Let's meet them:

Colette

She loves the color pink and wants to be a fashion writer. She's very particular about her appearance, which means she's always late!

Violet

She's a real intellectual, just like my brother, Geronimo. She likes to unwind by listening to classical music, and she wants to become a great violinist.

PAMELA

Give her a screwdriver and she can solve any mechanical problem. She loves pizza and would eat it for breakfast if she could!

PAULINA

This computer genius wants to be a scientist. She also loves traveling and meeting people from all over the world.

Nicky

She's always in a good mood as long as she's outdoors, in open spaces and nature. If she gets stuck in small, tight spaces, she gets claustrophobic.

THE CITY OF ATLANTIS

The Royal Palace

The Palace of the Ten Kings

The Coral Hills

The Royal Library

The Nautical Garden

The Ocean Door

During this adventure, you and the Thea Sisters will find clues that will lead you to the fantastic Kingdom of Atlantis. The names of the mysterious places there are hidden in some of the illustrations. To read them, you will need to hold the page up to a mirror.

VACATION TIME

Nice to meet you! My name is Thea Stilton. I'm a busy rodent these days, between writing articles for *The Rodent's Gazette* and teaching at Mouseford Academy. After a BUSY semester of teaching, I set off early for an OCEAN voyage. I love to travel the world!

Little did I know that while I was away, my dear friends the THEA SISTERS would stumble upon an AMAZING adventure. I'm sure you know all about the Thea Sisters — Colette, Nicky, PAMELA, PAULINA, and Violet were in my class at Mouseford Academy and are the five brightest young rodents I know!

When I returned from my trip, they called me for help, and I was happy to be part of such an incredible experience with them. Then I wrote down what happened to share with you, my loyal readers.

The Thea Sisters' tale begins at the start of the semester break. As much as they love their studies, they were all eager to go on vacations and have some fun.

The mouselets were making last-minute preparations, HURRYING to pack their backpacks and suitcases. But PAULINA was sitting peacefully on her bed, watching the others.

"Don't worry about me," she assured her friends. "I'll be fine!"

Nicky shook her head. "I don't understand how you can prefer the halls of Mouseford to a nice vacation in the open air!"

Nicky was returning home to Australia for a visit to the wide-open Outback.

2

Quiet **Violet** spoke up. "I would invite you to come to my music composition class, but I think you'd find it boring."

Paulina responded with a smile. "I'll be fine here, *relaxing*. Plus, **PROFESSOR SPARKLE** asked me to cross-check the dates of his research on **ANCIENT** civilizations."

"That seems . . . *HUFF* . . . like a lot of work . . . *PUFF*," said blonde *Colette*, who was trying to close her overstuffed PINK suitcase. "But nobody knows ancient civilizations better than you, Pauly. You're definitely the best mouse for the job!"

Paulina couldn't help smiling at Colette's battle with her suitcase. "Are you sure you need so many evening dresses for the beaches of the **CARIBBEAN**?" she asked.

"Don't joke!" Colette replied seriously. "I

already had to leave out three of my fur conditioners!"

"**Let's goooooooo!**"

PAM, the fifth Thea Sister, burst into the room like a *TORNADO*. She knocked over all of the suitcases and bags stacked by the door.

Paulina jumped to help pick up the bags.

"It's **late**!" Pam exclaimed. "Let's get *moving*, or we'll miss our hydroplane out of here."

"I can't close my bag!" Colette wailed.

"Leave it to me, Coco," Pam said. Then the sporty rodent LEAPED across the room and landed on Colette's bag.

CLICK!

"Come on, everyone!" Pam cried.

"**Our vacations await!**"

MYSTERY ON THE SHORE

Paulina watched her friends drive off until they disappeared over the horizon.

"Time to work!" she said, heading out of her room. "My research awaits!"

As Paulina walked down the deserted corridors of the academy to the library, she couldn't believe how quiet it was. The other students and professors had already left. Even the academy director, **PROFESSOR OCTAVIUS DE MOUSUS**, had traveled to the other side of the island to give a speech.

In the large LIBRARY, the afternoon sunlight shone through the windows and a peaceful silence filled the space. Paulina took a seat at one of the computer stations and began to work. She was so absorbed in her task that when she finally looked up from her screen she saw **STARS** shimmering in the sky.

Paulina shut down her computer and stretched. "What I need is a **LiGHt DinneR** and a **GOOD NIGHT'S SLEEP**!" she said happily. She returned to her room and enjoyed some cream of cheese soup. Before she fell asleep, she set her alarm clock so she could get an early start on her research the next morning.

BOOM! Paulina woke up from her sound sleep with a start. It was still dark outside, and a pouring rain pounded at the windows. A flash of **LIGHTNING** lit up the room, followed by another **rumble** of thunder that seemed to shake the walls.

"What a terrible **storm**!" Paulina whispered, pulling her covers up to her chin.

It was a little **SCARY** to be alone in the room, without her friends by her side.

The storm seemed to rage for hours as the rain fell like buckets of cheese sauce and the thunder boomed. It wasn't easy, but Paulina finally fell into a Light and **restless** sleep.

When her alarm clock rang shortly after sunrise, Paulina groaned as she shut it off.

She was exhausted! But at least the storm was over. She opened her window and the **fResH aiR** perked her right up.

"A **JOG** on the beach is just what I need," she told herself, and she put on some exercise clothes. Then she went to the kitchen to grab some food before her run.

Midge Whale, the academy's cook, had a glass of fresh orange juice ready for her.

"Did you hear that storm last night?" Midge asked. "It's been years since we've had a **storm** like that!"

Paulina chatted with Midge as she downed her breakfast, then jogged to the beach. She **gasped** as the ocean came into view. Instead of its usual sky-blue color, the water was an intense **DeeP BLUe** streaked with green. The sky was a misty gray color, and the **SAND**, still damp, was strewn with branches and seaweed.

She broke into a run, and her steps sank into the wet sand. The morning sunlight sparkled on the waves, and seagulls flew overhead.

The view was so **Beautiful** that Paulina slowed down to enjoy it. That's when she spotted a large object against the dark sand just up ahead. It almost looked like some

kind of plant, except it was **blue**.

Is it an animal? she wondered. But what kind? Maybe a large fish?

As Paulina got closer, she realized that the object definitely wasn't a PLANT. She quickened her pace as a sense of alarm swept through her body. Her *heart* beat faster as the silhouette of the object became clear. This was no fish, either. . . .

A STRANGER FROM THE SEA

Paulina was so **shocked** that she couldn't move. A strange boy with *blue* skin was lying in the sand with his eyes closed. He had long BLUE hair, and he wore a yellow tunic that looked like it was speckled with real gold. The boy reminded Paulina of one of the characters in a fairy tale that she had read to her little sister.

Cautiously, Paulina approached him. He wasn't moving at all, even though the WAVES were lapping at his legs. He had a tranquil expression on his face, as though he were sleeping.

"Excuse me, are you all right?" Paulina asked, but the boy didn't answer her. She began to fear that something was really wrong.

She knelt down and placed her paw on his tunic. Beneath the fabric she could feel a BEATING heart! She sighed with relief and tried to wake him again.

The boy didn't open his eyes; he seemed to have fainted. Paulina got up and scanned the area for a **boat** or raft that might have brought him there. But she couldn't spot anything — not even wreckage.

She gazed at the boy again, transfixed. *Where had he come from?* she wondered. His blue skin seemed to **glow**, and when she touched the fabric of his tunic, it was impossibly soft. And his face looked so kind.

She quickly snapped out of her thoughts. Whoever this boy was, he needed help. SHE COULDN'T WASTE ANOTHER SECOND!

Paulina ran into town as fast as she could. As she crossed the bridge, she almost bumped into Elly Squid, her classmate, who lived on WHALE ISLAND.

"Are you trying to break some kind of **SPEED** record?" Elly teased.

"Oh, Elly . . . **HUFF**! You must . . . **PUFF** . . . help me!" Paulina panted as she caught her breath. "I went running on the beach, and I found a boy!"

"You met a **boy**?" her friend asked, confused.

"No!" Paulina cried. "I didn't meet him. I **FOUND** him!"

Poor Elly was perplexed.

"He's a castaway," Paulina explained.

Elly's eyes grew wide. "A **castaway**? How is he? Where did he come from? What did he say to you?"

"He didn't say anything," Paulina replied. "He's passed out!"

"I know just the rodent who can help us," Elly said. Then she yelled, "**LEOPOLD!**"

Leopold Whale, an accomplished sailor and fishermouse, popped his snout out of his house window.

"Hi, Elly! What's up?" he asked.

Paulina and Elly quickly filled him in and the three of them *RACED* to the beach. The boy with **BLUE** skin was exactly where Paulina had found him, and he still looked fast asleep.

Leopold and Elly were amazed.

"His skin really seems to GLOW," whispered Elly, enchanted.

"He looks almost magical, somehow," Leopold mused. "But we can't just stand here and stare at him. Let's get him to a DOCTOR!"

SO MANY
MYSTERIES . . .

Leopold and Paulina carried the **strange** boy to Mouseford Academy and *gently* placed him on a bed in one of the empty rooms. Elly ran to fetch the school doctor. He quietly examined the patient.

"He's simply SLEEPING very deeply," the doctor announced a few minutes later. "You just need to keep him WARM and wait for him to wake up. Who is he?"

"We don't know," Paulina replied.

"He doesn't even have a wallet," Leopold added. "Or a phone."

All four rodents were quiet for a moment. Then the doctor felt the edge of the GOLDEN tunic.

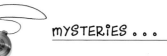
"I've only encountered fabric like this in a mouseum," he said thoughtfully. "But it's so unusual, there's no mistaking it. THIS TUNIC IS MADE OF SEA SILK!"

"What is that?" Paulina asked.

"It is a very rare fabric made from the fibers from a kind of **mollusk**," the doctor explained.

"You mean from a creature with a ꜱʜᴇʟʟ, like a clam or a mussel?" asked Leopold the fishermouse.

"Exactly!" the doctor cried. "These fibers are even FINER than silk, and the fabric is light, yet **warm**. It is quite precious."

"So this must be someone very **important**!" Leopold guessed.

The doctor nodded. "Perhaps," he said. "It's strange, though—**SEA SILK** hasn't been produced anywhere for many years."

"How **odd**," Elly said.

"Well, there's nothing more I can do now," the doctor said. "Watch over him, and contact me if anything changes."

He and Leopold left, but Paulina and Elly stayed behind with the sleeping stranger. They were quiet for a moment.

"What an unusual necklace he has," Elly remarked.

Paulina leaned over to look. Strung around the boy's neck was a **blue** stone set in a circle of **RED METAL**. The back of the stone was embossed with an ʊᴎʊsʊɒʟ circular design.

Curious, Paulina reached out to touch the medallion, and at the same moment, the boy's eyelids **FLUTTERED**. He began to speak in a soft WHISPER, but the words were in a LANGUAGE she had never heard before. Then his eyes closed again and he fell back to sleep.

"WHAT DID HE SAY?" Elly asked.

Paulina shook her head. "I didn't understand him. Did you?"

"It sounded more like music than words," Elly remarked.

Paulina was more puzzled than ever.

"This is too much for just us to handle," she said.

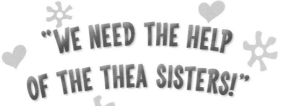

"WE NEED THE HELP OF THE THEA SISTERS!"

FRIENDS TO THE RESCUE

"HELLO? HELLO? PAULY, CAN YOU HEAR ME?"

"Colette? Is that you?"

"Yes, but I'm about to board a plane for the **CARIBBEAN**," Colette replied. "I spent an hour at the baggage checkpoint. They tried to stop me from bringing my **BOTTLES** of conditioning cream. Don't they know the importance of well-maintained **fur**?"

At the other end of the phone, Paulina smiled. But there was no time to **CHAT** about fur styling.

"Coco, I'm sorry, but there's an *EMERGENCY* here," she said. She quickly explained the situation to her friend.

"It's very **MYSTERIOUS**," Paulina said. "He woke up and uttered some incomprehensible words. But then he went back to sleep!"

"Well, of course he's **TIRED**—he just got shipwrecked," Colette replied.

Paulina sighed. "He doesn't have any identification on him, except for a strange **JEWEL** around his neck. I really don't know what to do!"

Colette looked at the boarding pass in her paws. Her **plane** was going to take off in ten minutes. She closed her eyes and imagined

the white beaches and clear waters of the Caribbean. But Paulina sounded so **worried** that she knew what she had to do.

"All right," she agreed. "I can be back at Mouseford tomorrow."

"Oh, thank you, Colette!" Paulina cried with relief.

"Have you told the others yet?" Colette asked.

"No," Paulina replied. "I was about to call **Violet**. . . ."

"Then I'll call PAM and *Nicky*," Colette said. "I'll see you at the academy. Once we're all **together** we can figure this out!"

By the next day, all of the THEA SISTERS were back on Whale Island.

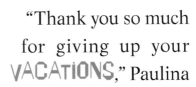

"Thank you so much for giving up your VACATIONS," Paulina

said **gratefully** as she led her friends down the hallway.

"Someone is in trouble, and there's a **MYSTERY** to solve. We couldn't say no!" Nicky said firmly.

Colette nodded. "That's right. And besides . . ."

But she stopped midsentence as Paulina opened the door to the boy's room. The other Thea Sisters gasped as they saw the boy with the **BLUE SKIN** for the first time.

The sleeping boy looked as though he had been carved from **ice**. His face was perfectly still, with a **peaceful** expression. The only sign of life was the slow movement of his chest, which rose up and fell down in a steady rhythm.

"I'm worried," Paulina said. "The doctor said he's a bit **weaker** than yesterday."

Pam moved in to get a **closer** look. "Weaker?"

"Yes, his heartbeat has slowed and his skin is less bright," Paulina explained.

"Bright? What do you mean?" Pam asked.

Paulina started to explain about the **glow** the boy had when she first found him on the beach. While she talked, Nicky leaned in closer to touch his **medallion**.

"How beautiful," she whispered.

Suddenly, the boy began to stir, and his **EYES** opened slowly. Nicky jumped in shock.

The room was quiet as everyone watched to see what the boy would do next. The stranger began to talk in his strange, **musical** language. Confusion filled his eyes when he saw the Thea Sisters around him. He tried to sit up, but he was too **weak**. He collapsed into the pillows and closed his eyes again.

"Oh, no! Not again! You need to stay awake," Pam said, lightly shaking his shoulders.

Paulina was scared. "PAM, WHAT ARE YOU DOING?" she cried.

But she relaxed when the boy opened his eyes again.

"That's more like it!" Pam exclaimed.

She helped him sit up in the bed, and the other Thea Sisters began to talk all at once.

"What he needs is a sip of some herbal tea," Violet suggested.

"Or maybe a relaxing bath with some essential oils," said Colette.

Nicky shook her head. "Air! He needs some fresh air!"

"I'm going to cook him a nice pizza," offered Pam.

"Shhh!" Paulina warned. Then she looked right into the boy's EYES. "Why don't we ask *him* what we should do?"

THE UNIVERSAL LANGUAGE

Everyone was quiet for a moment. Then Pam asked, "How are we going to **COMMUNICATE** with him? We don't understand anything he says."

"And from the way he's looking at us, I would say he's having the same problem," Nicky added.

They all thought for a moment.

"Maybe we could ACT OUT what we're trying to say," Paulina suggested.

The mouselets gave it their best shot, but acting out questions like "Who are you?" and "Where are you from?" wasn't easy.

"Maybe he's weak from hunger," Pam guessed, so they asked Midge Whale to make some **macaroni and cheese**. But even though the Thea Sisters thought the food smelled delicious, the boy just looked at it with **SAD** eyes.

"Maybe where he's from they eat different food," Violet mused out loud. "When I first moved here I had a **DIFFICULT** time getting used to the **FLAVORS** that were so different than the food I grew up with in China."

"I knew we should have gone with a pizza!" Pam said. "It's the most international food in the world."

"What if he doesn't like it?" Paulina asked.

"EVERYONE likes pizza," Pam insisted.

"I've got it!" Colette exclaimed, running out of the room. When she returned, she was holding a pad and some colored pencils. "He can **draw** for us."

The blue stranger seemed to understand

immediately what the mouselets wanted him to do and he reached for the notebook. After a few seconds, he showed them what he had drawn: a few LiNes that looked like the WAVY surface of the sea.

Nicky frowned. "Yes, we know you come from the sea," she said with a sigh.

But Violet had a different idea. "Wait," she said, turning to the blue-skinned boy. "Fish? Do you want fish to eat?" With her paws, she made a motion of eating something.

The boy drew some DARK GREEN lines underneath the waves.

"Grass? Plants?" Pam guessed.

"Algae," Violet murmured. "He wants **algae**!"

Midge Whale frowned thoughtfully. "Well, I could try to make some algae soup," she said, and hurried off.

Colette smiled triumphantly. "Art is the universal language! See? It worked!"

"Let's keep using it," Paulina suggested.

She took the pad from the boy and began to draw some more ocean WAVES. Then she drew big, dark **clouds** in the sky and streaks of lightning. Finally, she filled the page with lines to represent the heavy RAIN.

"Do you remember this **storm**?" she asked the stranger, pointing to the picture.

He nodded and took the pad from her, adding a tiny figure to the water.

"So he did come from the 𝕊𝕖𝕒, just as you thought," Nicky commented. She took the pad and drew the outline of a **house**.

"Where do you live?" she asked.

The stranger looked at her for a moment, and then he turned his head away, avoiding eye contact with any of them.

"He didn't understand that one," Pam said.

"Or maybe he doesn't want to tell us," added Colette **thoughtfully**.

IN A
STRANGE LAND

The boy with the blue skin waited until the Thea Sisters left the room. Then he slowly got out of bed and walked to the window to look outside.

His heart was filled with confused emotions and his head was a whirlwind of thoughts. Only the rigorous training he had received as a child allowed him to stay in control.

He had been right all along. A world did exist out here, beyond the surface of the sea. It was very similar to the one described in legends that his people kept in the Room of Frozen Words.

For years, the people who lived in his

faraway kingdom had believed that what was written in those precious volumes were just stories. Myths. But they were wrong. The legends were real, and he had proved it.

"If only you could see this world through my eyes, Father," the boy murmured. "You wouldn't call me a dreamer anymore!"

He stared at the garden outside the window, which was unlike any garden he had ever seen. It was so green and bright! All those plants and the trees that swayed in the wind . . . they made his eyes spin.

And oh, the wind! He had never felt it before, the sweet caress of the wind on his face. It was an incredible feeling, one that he would never forget.

Then his mood darkened, thinking of the storm that had shipwrecked him a few days before. He shivered as the memories brought a chill to his body. He thought of the boat that had brought him to the surface of the sea, how it had tossed and turned in the angry waves.

He felt sad as he thought about all the things he had lost. His precious instruments,

all of his food, even the portrait of his beloved family. It was all gone, lost forever in the depths of the ocean.

He remembered waking up here, in the world above sea level, the world that nobody except him believed was real. At first, everything around him seemed so complicated, with too many colors and too many noises for him to understand.

And he felt different here. Walking just a few steps tired him out. His bones felt heavy and his muscles felt weak. The language of the mice who had helped him stung his ears. And if he looked up, he got dizzy. The sky was the most sensational thing he had ever seen!

"I think you would like this place very much, little sister," he murmured in his melodious language. Then he bit his lip in fear. Would he ever see his beloved sister, Astra, again? Would he ever be able to go home?

An image of Astra came to him, with her long blue hair that was soft like algae, and the gentle twinkle of her green eyes. He could almost hear the beautiful echoes of the melodies she played on her harp.

At first, he had regretted not bringing her on this journey. But perhaps it was for the best. Only a miracle had allowed him to survive the storm. At least Astra was home, safe.

The thought made him smile, and he clutched the medallion around his neck and went back to bed.

I am a stranger in a strange land, *he thought as he drifted back to sleep.*

THE NAUTICAL
GARDEN

AN UNEXPECTED RETURN

The news that a **strange** boy with **BLUE SKIN** had been found quickly spread across Whale Island. In no time, it had reached the ears of a Mouseford student who had recently landed in Mexico in her private helicopter: *Ruby Flashyfur*.

Ruby came from a wealthy family, and was always competing with the Thea Sisters. She hated for anyone else to be the **CENTER** of attention. So when she left for vacation, she asked her personal assistant, Alan, to stay and observe for her.

Alan was **BORED** at first. The only other rodent in sight was the quiet mouseling with the long black braid. But on the third day, he was **surprised** when the other Thea Sisters returned. He followed them and was **amazed** at what he saw. He called Ruby right away.

"A **stranger**? What kind of stranger?" Ruby squawked into her MousePhone.

"Well, I'm not sure," Alan replied. "The Thea Sisters are taking care of him. He's quite unusual."

"You're not making any sense!" Ruby yelled, frustrated. It really bugged her that the Thea Sisters were involved in something interesting.

"Well, he has **BLUE** hair and **BLUE** skin," Alan explained.

"Stop lying!" Ruby said crossly.

"It's the truth!" Alan insisted.

"**INTERESTING**," Ruby murmured

as she hung up the phone. Then she hopped back on her private helicopter and headed right back to Mouseford Academy.

In the meantime, the Thea Sisters had been trying everything they could think of to cure the boy with the **BLUE** skin. He had a sweet smile and a gentle way about him that had won all of them over, including Midge. The cook had prepared him every algae recipe she could find. Thankfully, he seemed to be slowly getting STRONGER.

The Thea Sisters continued using PICTURES to communicate, but they still could not figure out where the boy had come from.

"It's a real mystery, all right," Nicky commented as she headed down to the port with Paulina and Violet. They wanted to look at the list of **boats** that had sailed near the island on the night of the storm. But when they arrived, they were **surprised** to see the Flashyfur family yacht anchored there.

"**Ruby's back?**" Paulina asked.

Nicky looked puzzled. "I thought she was in Mexico." Violet frowned. "I'll bet the **REASON** she's back early is related to our friend with the **BLUE** skin."

"But how could she know about him?" Nicky wondered, as *Ruby* came down the dock.

"**Yoo-hoo! Darlings!** How good to see you!" Ruby called out to them.

The three mice were stunned. Ruby had never been **NICE** to them before.

"Hi, Ruby," Paulina said. "Why are you back so early?"

"Oh, Mexico is beautiful, but after a while everything becomes so **boring**," she said. "Plus, I missed school and my *friends*."

"Is Ruby talking about us?" Nicky WHiSPeReD to Violet.

"Now," Ruby continued, "I know that you

have a new friend. You didn't intend to keep him to yourself, did you?"

She flashed them a **CRAFTY** smile.

Violet rolled her eyes. "What did I tell you?" she muttered to her friends. "A Flashyfur is never nice without a motive!"

LEAVE HiM TO ME!

Ruby bombarded the three Thea Sisters with *questions* as they walked back to Mouseford.

"Did you find out where he's from? Is it true that he wears **golden** clothes? Is he a **NOBLEMAN**?"

Nicky, Paulina, and Violet didn't have many answers to give her, but Ruby didn't give up. When she found out what room the boy was staying in, she ran off.

Pam and Colette were in the boy's room when their friends got back.

"We have news," Paulina said with a sigh.

"**GUESS WHO** just arrived on the island," Nicky said.

Before anyone could guess, Ruby pranced

into the room wearing an *elegant* and expensive-looking PINK dress with perfectly styled hair. She had obviously gotten dressed up to meet the stranger.

"Ruby!" Pam and Colette cried.

Ruby walked straight to the boy. "Esteemed guest, it is a great honor to have you in our humble school!"

She held out her paw so that he could *kiss* it. But the boy just stared, stunned.

"A-hem!" Ruby loudly cleared her throat, hoping the boy would take the hint. When he didn't, she reluctantly lowered her paw.

"A special guest like yourself should not be in any old room. I INSIST that you stay on our family yacht," she told him.

"I'm afraid he doesn't understand our language," Paulina informed her. "And I

don't think he's interested in your yacht!"

"Nonsense!" Ruby sniffed. She grabbed the boy's arm. "Now, come with me!"

She pulled the confused boy out of his bed and dragged him from the room. The Thea Sisters followed. Once Ruby set her mind on something, it was hard to stop her!

"We can't let her **take** him!" Pam cried.

"There's not much we can do," Violet said with a sigh. "Ruby will take care of him in her own way. At least we can focus on solving the **mystery** of where he's from."

Colette's blue eyes **lit up**. "I have an idea!" she cried. "We should call someone who is SMART, well-connected, well-traveled, and is always ready to HELP us. Do you know who I'm talking about?"

"Thea Stilton, of course!" the others shouted in unison.

HELP FROM THEA

That same day, I, Thea Stilton, had just returned from my **OCEAN** voyage. I had spent an entire week on a ship, researching whales and how they communicate with one another.

Even though I had to unpack all of my **LUGGAGE**, it was more important for me to **organize** all the notes I had taken on the trip. I needed to get working on an **ARTICLE** for *The Rodent's Gazette*, where I work as a **SPECIAL REPORTER**. My brother, Geronimo, is the editor of the paper, and he was anxious to

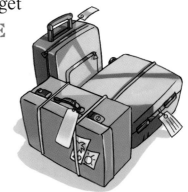

publish the piece.

I prepared a nice cup of tea and sat down at my desk to get to work, when . . .

Riiing! Riiing!

The sound of the phone made me jump. *Can that be Geronimo already?* I wondered. He usually knew to give me some PEACE while I was writing.

I picked up the receiver and immediately recognized the voice of PAULINA. I quickly guessed that the Thea Sisters might be involved in another of their adventures. Those mouselets are always up to something exciting!

"PAULINA! So nice to hear from you," I said. "Are the Thea Sisters away on another mystery-solving trip?"

"This time it's a little different, Thea," she replied. "The mystery came to us!"

Paulina sounded very serious, which made me a little worried — and very CURIOUS, I must admit. Then she told me all about the mysterious BLUE-SKINNED boy who had washed up onshore.

Colette took the phone from Paulina. "He's so **Fascinating**!" she told me.

The mouselets took turns talking, each one eager to tell me new details.

"He doesn't speak our language — his language sounds like singing," said Violet.

"And he eats algae!" Pam added.

"His tunic is made of Sea Silk and flecked with gold!" exclaimed Nicky.

Paulina calmed everyone down. "As you may have guessed, we are in a bit of TROUBLE," she confessed. "We communicate with him using drawings, but we can't understand much. It's like he landed on the beach from **ANOTHER WORLD!**"

The **wheels** in my brain were turning as my students talked. Their story was truly *incredible* — but yet, strangely familiar to me.

"Keep taking good care of him," I told them. "I will come to Mouseford as soon as possible. I might have something that can help you solve this **MYSTERY**."

I hung up the phone and walked into the living room. There, I removed a picture hanging from the wall, revealing a safe hidden behind it. I opened the safe and smiled. The **envelope** I needed was still there.

A HAPPENING PARTY

Ruby didn't waste any time. After dragging the boy with the **BLUE SKIN** onto her family yacht, she immediately got on the phone to prepare a fabumouse *PARTY* in his honor.

She planned every last detail: fresh flowers, sophisticated food, a few select guests, and of course, a **glamorous** gown for herself. She imagined how fascinating she would look with the castaway on her arm.

In reality, though, the boy didn't fascinate her that much. He didn't seem interested in the yacht at all, and seemed to miss the THEA SISTERS. But Ruby didn't worry too much. Surely the party would **CHEER** him up!

Ruby had reluctantly invited the THEA SISTERS to the party. Everyone knew that Paulina had found the castaway, and it would seem rude to exclude them.

The Thea Sisters decided to SPLIT UP the group that night. Paulina and Pam would stay at the academy and wait for Thea. The others would go to the PARTY and keep an eye on the boy with the blue skin.

That night, Nicky, Colette, and Violet boarded the yacht. Ruby stood in the center of the deck wearing a fancy green dress. She held her rather confused guest by the arm.

"Look at that!" exclaimed Colette. "Ruby is putting him on display like a TROPHY!"

Nicky scowled. "I almost regret leaving him in her paws. What do you think, Violet?"

But Violet didn't answer. She was distracted by two strange

rodents dressed in black, who were scanning the scene with great interest.

"Who are those guys?" Violet asked. "They don't look familiar."

"Don't mind them, Violet. They're probably bodyguards," Colette guessed. "Check out these beautiful **party favors** from Ruby!"

She happily took a **PINK** phone from the gift basket. "She has **good taste** this time!"

But Violet and Nicky weren't interested in **GIFTS**. They had approached Ruby, who was chatting with Princess Annabella Ratanoff.

"Excuse me, *Ruby*," Violet began.

"What is it?" Ruby snapped, **annoyed**.

"We just have a question.

Who are those two?" Nicky asked, pointing to the two rodents in black.

Ruby smiled smugly. "You mean **PROFESSOR QUASAR** and his assistant? He is a very famouse scientist! He studies **WHALE** migration, and he's here to make a documentary. My family is sharing our equipment with him, and he promised to put me in his film!"

Assistant

Professor Quasar

DANGER ON THE YACHT

The two **MOUSELETS** left Ruby with the princess and looked at each other, perplexed.

"If this Quasar really is a FAMOUSE scientist, why didn't he ask **PROFESSOR VAN KRAKEN** for help with his project?" Violet wondered.

"Good point," Nicky agreed. "Our professor is a marine biology expert with very advanced equipment."

Colette rushed up to them. "Forget about those men in black for now. I think we have an EMERGENCY!"

She pointed across the deck to the boy with the blue skin, who was leaning against the railing and looking very ill. When he

saw the Thea Sisters coming toward him he forced a WEAK smile. They quickly gathered around him.

"WE SHOULD GET HIM BACK TO THE SCHOOL RIGHT AWAY!" Nicky exclaimed. "All this confusion seems to be making him sick."

She and Colette each took one of his arms and they began to walk over the bridge leading to the dock. But a shrill voice made them JUMP.

"Where are you going?" It was Professor

Quasar, who was at the end of the bridge, **BLOCKING** their way.

"Our friend isn't feeling well," Colette said firmly. "We're taking him to a calmer place."

Professor Quasar's expression changed to a slimy smile. He walked up to them.

"Why don't I have a **LOOK**? I'm a **DOCTOR**," he said.

"A doctor?" murmured Violet, who had caught up to them. Wasn't he a scientist?

At that moment, Colette screamed. The boy with the blue skin had fainted and was **SLIDING** to the ground, slipping through their arms.

Ruby heard Colette's **YELL** and quickly ran up to them. "What have you done to him?" she accused.

"Air! Give him some air!" someone yelled.

"A glass of water, quick!" shouted another rodent.

The party guests crowded around the boy, *SHOVING* the Thea Sisters aside. When they managed to get close again, the boy was opening his eyes. At the same time, Violet noticed Professor Quasar leaving **QUICKLY**.

Such a strange character, she thought.

The boy was back on his feet, and he linked arms with Nicky. Ruby immediately began to insist that he return to the yacht.

"Ruby, he needs to get back to the school," Nicky said in a voice like **S T E E L**, and Ruby knew she had lost.

"All right, then! Let our party continue without our BLUE guest!" she announced in a fake cheerful voice. Then she leaned in to the Thea Sisters.

"Go ahead and take him. But this doesn't end here!" she warned.

They ignored her and headed to the dock. Then Colette stopped.

"Hold on! I lost my purse!" she exclaimed in alarm.

She had just turned to go back to the yacht when a PAW extended in front of her, holding a small PURPLE clutch.

"Is it this one?" asked Professor Quasar's assistant. He seemed to have popped out of nowhere.

"Yes, thanks, but how—"

Before Colette could finish her question, the assistant DiSAPPeaReD.

CAUGHT IN A TRAP!

When Nicky, Colette, and Violet returned to the school that evening, they found me waiting for them with Paulina and Pamela.

"Thea! You're here!" Nicky exclaimed, and all three mouselets rushed up to hug me.

The first thing we did was take the blue-skinned boy back to his room. He collapsed into a **DEEP** sleep as soon as he hit the bed.

Then we gathered in Paulina's room, where Violet told us what had happened. She described the two strange guests to us.

"The name **QUASAR** doesn't ring any bells for me," I commented. "I just finished working with a team of **SCIENTISTS** who study whale migration. I didn't know anyone else was doing similar research."

"Who knows where he comes from," Colette added. "It's another **mystery**!"

I nodded in agreement. "On that note, I have something that might help with your first mystery. But I think we all need some sleep right now. Let's talk in the **morning**."

As tired as we all were, the Thea Sisters took turns all night **WATCHING** over the boy, who groaned as if he had a **fever**.

As they ate BREAKFAST at dawn, Colette yawned. "What a hard night! Not even an intensive cucumber mask would help the bags under my eyes!"

"And our friend is getting **worse**," said a worried Violet.

"We should call the doctor," proposed Nicky.

"I don't know what he can do," Paulina said with a sigh. "Until we know more about the boy, we can't **HELP** him."

The mouselings exchanged frustrated glances. They felt TiReD and anxious. After they ate, Nicky suggested they take a walk outside, and the FRESH AIR relaxed them immediately. The garden was an explosion of colors and scents.

Violet was smelling some *flowers* when a voice from the bushes startled them.

"Good morning, Thea Sisters!"

"Boomer?" asked Violet as Boomer Whale popped up from behind a bush.

"What are you doing back there?" Paulina asked.

"Weeding the garden," he replied. "But I was just about to call you. Some RODENT just passed through here looking for you."

"What was his name?" Nicky asked suspiciously.

"It was, um, Lasar . . . no, Fasar?" Boomer replied, scratching his head.

"QUASAR?" suggested Nicky.

"Exactly!" Boomer cried. "He said something about a MEDALLION, and that he's

69

waiting for you in the library. He seemed really out of it. He didn't even know which way the library was!"

"Thanks, Boomer. We'll go see him RIGHT NOW," Paulina declared.

The Thea Sisters rushed to the library, curious to know what the mysterious rodent was up to. They found that the library door was slightly open, and they ran inside the room. It was EMPTY.

"Professor Quasar? Are you here?" Nicky called out. THERE WAS NO ANSWER.

Then Paulina spotted a hat that looked like Professor Quasar's sticking out over a chair in the corner.

"PROFESSOR?" she asked.

There was still no answer. The mouselets cautiously approached the chair. But when they got to it, they realized that the hat was just propped up by **BOOKS**—and not on Professor Quasar's head.

"What sort of joke is this?" asked Violet. **BAM!** The library door **SLAMMED** shut behind them, and there was a loud **CLICK**. Someone had locked them inside!

THE MYSTERIOUS ENVELOPE

They were quiet for a moment as they realized what had happened.

Then Nicky yelled, "**We're in a trap!**"

"I don't like this one bit!" Pam cried.

"Take a deep breath, everyone," Colette advised, trying to calm her friends. "We'll get out of here. Pam, can you use my hairpin to pick the lock?"

"GREAT IDEA!" Pam agreed. She took the pin and began to work on the lock.

"Hmm," she said after a while. "It's not as easy as it looks in the movies."

They were all starting to worry again when I called to them from behind the door. "Thea Sisters? Are you in there?"

"Thea! Yes! We're locked in!" Nicky yelled.

"Hang on! I'll help you," I told them.

I quickly found the custodian and got a copy of the library **key**. When I unlocked the door, the mouselets rushed out, grateful and relieved.

"**WHat HappeneD?**" I asked them. "I looked for you everywhere. **Luckily** I ran into Boomer, who told me that you had come here."

"Professor Quasar told Boomer that he was waiting for us in the library," Paulina explained. "But he tricked us!"

"Why would he do that?" I wondered.

Paulina suddenly turned pale. "What if he means to hurt the blue-skinned boy?"

"Don't worry about him; he's safe," I assured them. "Boomer just picked him up and took him to the doctor. As soon as they come back, we're getting him out of here. I've already booked a flight."

"To where?" the mouselets asked at once.

"BUENOS AIRES!" I announced.

They looked at one another, stunned.

I grinned. "Follow me and I'll explain."

We went to my room and I took a large envelope from my suitcase. A letter was clipped to the front.

"Your story of the mysterious castaway reminded me of a letter that I received from an old classmate of mine named Kelly. I think it's time to share it with you."

I read the letter to the Thea Sisters.

Dearest Thea,

I'm sorry I haven't written to you in so long! Unfortunately, my new job forces me to be very secretive. I can only tell you that I work on mysteries. I know that you often find yourself involved in puzzling cases, so I decided to give you a special gift.

If you ever encounter a mystery so challenging that there does not seem to be a solution, fly immediately to Buenos Aires, Argentina. Once you get there, open the envelope attached to this letter and you will find secret information that will help you.

I hope to see you again one day, my friend!

Yours, Kelly

ANOTHER TRAP

While the Thea Sisters prepared for the trip, Boomer and I **searched** the deserted school for Professor Quasar. I feared that Paulina's **SUSPICIONS** were right, and he was after the **BLUE-SKINNED** boy. So I devised a plan to distract him while the Thea Sisters and the boy left Whale Island.

We walked all the way up to the school's North Tower, where we heard **muffled** noises coming from the very top. I climbed a few more steps and bumped into a young rodent in dark clothing.

"**Good morning!**" I said cheerfully. "You must be Professor Quasar."

"A-actually, I'm his **ASSISTANT**," the rodent stammered, taken by surprise.

"I am Thea Stilton. I teach ADVENTURE journalism, and I just finished some research on **whale** migration routes," I said. "I understand that you and Professor Quasar are also studying this. I'd love to **SHARE** my information with you."

Quasar's assistant was obviously embarrassed.

"Y-yes, maybe one of these days," he said. "We're very busy right now."

"Of course," I replied.

"We're busy as well."

Boomer winked at me. "Yes, the boy with the **BLUE** skin is waiting for us in the astronomy observatory," he said in a loud, clear voice.

At those words the assistant lit up—just like I knew he would.

"I really am in quite a hurry," he said. "Good-bye!"

Then he *RUSHED* off.

I smiled. Our plan was working perfectly!

"Ha! I think he bought it," Boomer said. "Now we just have to see if he tells the professor."

Boomer and I secretly kept an eye on the assistant, and he did just as we thought. A few minutes later, he and Professor Quasar were **TRUDGING** up the hill to the observatory.

"There's no time to lose!" Quasar

barked at his assistant, who was huffing and puffing. "We've got him right in our paws!"

But when they burst through the observatory door, they found an **EMPTY ROOM**. They turned over every telescope, but there wasn't a trace of the boy with the blue skin. Then the assistant opened a closet filled with old books, and one fell on the professor's head.

"I-I'm sorry, professor," the assistant stuttered nervously.

"We're wasting our time!" Professor Quasar said crossly. "Let's go back to the library and question those five meddlesome students."

But when they got to the library, there was no sign of the THEA SISTERS.

"You can't do anything right!" Quasar angrily yelled at his assistant. "YOU'RE FIRED!"

Then the professor smiled WICKEDLY.

"If those mouselets think they can get rid of me so easily, they don't know how WRONG they are!" he murmured.

FIRST STOP: ARGENTINA!

While Boomer and I distracted Professor Quasar, the Thea Sisters and the boy with the **BLUE SKIN** quickly made their way to the dock to catch a ferry to the mainland. From there, they headed straight to the airport. The busy terminal was crowded with rodents, and the boy looked **UNEASY**. He stuck close to the mouselets as they checked their luggage and boarded the plane.

Paulina sat next to the boy.

"Don't worry," she said, even though she knew he didn't understand. "We're going to find someone who can help us."

"Let's open the envelope!" Colette cried once the plane took off. Her voice was filled with excitement — and a little fear.

Violet took the envelope out, and found exactly one sheet of paper inside. The Thea Sisters gathered around her and read the **message** together.

CAREFULLY LOOK AROUND. THE TOWER'S APPEARANCE IS DECEIVING!

The Thea Sisters looked at one another, **confused**. The message wasn't very clear.

"Maybe we need to look for this tower in

Argentina," Colette mused.

"Or maybe there's a **CODE** of some kind in the clue," Violet suggested. "Let's study it."

Pam took a **cheese** sandwich from her bag. "I can't study on an empty stomach!"

Pam leaned over her seat to look at the message. She took a bite just as the plane **jolted** in the air, and Pam lurched forward. Some **SPICY SAUCE** slopped from her sandwich onto the letter.

"Sorry!" Pam cried. She held out a napkin to clean it.

"It's no use." Violet sighed. "The paper is stained. You can hardly read it anymore."

Paulina looked thoughtful. "I think I just discovered the code!" She took the letter. "Look, the stain has left only each word's INITIAL LETTER visible!"

"So if you put the first letter of each line into one word, it spells *CLATTAI*," Colette added.

"What does that mean?" Pam asked.

"*C* could stand for *calle*, which means 'street' in Spanish," Paulina guessed. "*Latta* could be the name of the street."

"And *I* could stand for the number one—the building number!" Nicky finished. "Pauly, you're a genius!"

85

BETWEEN THE CLOUDS

During the flight, the blue-skinned boy silently stared out the window. Not long ago, he had entered the belly of a giant metal vehicle. When he sat down and looked outside, he saw a long strip of black asphalt stretching in front of them. Was this some road they were going to travel?

When the doors closed, he felt as though he were back in the ship that had taken him away from his home. For a moment, his thoughts drifted far away, all the way to his kingdom hidden in the depths of the sea . . . Atlantis. This was the land of his people, the land where he was born. And now he wasn't sure if he would ever be able to return.

The vehicle rumbled, waking him from his daydream. It moved faster and faster, and the boy noticed the metal wings attached to the craft. He had no idea what to expect.

As the craft raced even more quickly, the boy smiled, despite the sadness in his heart. It reminded him of afternoons he had spent in Atlantis with his sister, Astra. They would race down the steep slopes of the Coral Hills in a horse-drawn carriage on their way to the Palace of the Ten Kings. His sister's wavy blue hair would dance on her shoulders as the carriage picked up speed.

And how she laughed! Astra loved the thrill, and he often encouraged her to spur on the horses so they would run even faster. The horses were quick and strong, but their speed was nothing compared to this metal

craft. The force pressed him back against his seat, leaving him breathless.

As he looked out the window, he noticed that the big winged vessel was rising from the ground. The craft began to soar upward, like some giant bird. He was flying!

Amazed, he watched through the window as everything on the ground became smaller and smaller. The streets looked like spider-webs, and the wavy coastline looked like it had been drawn by a child. The vast sea sparkled in the sunlight. The boy couldn't take his eyes off of it all.

He marveled at the imagination of the inhabitants of this strange world. They had invented a vehicle that could fly! He was sailing through the clouds—perfect wisps of white that stretched across the sky. There was nothing like them in Atlantis.

Yes, his kingdom had streets paved with gold, and the Upside-Down Tower, and other wonders. But right now, nothing compared to this sensation of flying.

He was lost in thought when he felt someone's eyes on him. He looked up to see Paulina smiling at him. She opened up a map and pointed to a tiny island.

"Mouseford," she said. "Mouseford."

He recognized that word—it was the place where he had washed ashore. He watched as Paulina's paw traced a line on the map across the ocean and landed on a large continent. Could this world really be so big?

Paulina pointed to one of the land areas outlined on the map, and said a melodious word: "Argentina."

THREE IMPORTANT HATS

As soon as the plane landed, the Thea Sisters **HURRIED** out of the airport and hailed a taxi.

"Calle Latta, number one, please!" Paulina told the driver.

The car *SPED OFF* into the heart of Buenos Aires. They navigated through the maze of the city until coming to a street that was practically hidden away. The driver stopped the car.

The mouselets thanked him and got out, feeling slightly CONFUSED. They expected to be at a detective agency or somewhere official-looking, but they found themselves in front of a HAT SHOP!

"Are we sure this is the right place?" Violet asked.

"The address and the **UNUSUAL** street name are right," said Pam.

"I'm not so sure," Paulina said warily, but then the boy gave her an encouraging smile.

"Well, we did come all this way. We might as well check it out!" She said, smiling back.

Inside the shop, they were greeted with an explosion of **COLORS** and shapes. Shelves and tables held hats of every style. There were feathers, flowers, ribbons, veils, pom-poms, and more. The Thea Sisters stared at the spectacle, wide-eyed.

A voice snapped them back to their mission. "Hello!"

They didn't see anyone, but behind the counter a nest of branches holding a live **robin** had popped up. When the nest rose higher, underneath it they saw a round, **Friendly** face with **Smiling** eyes. The mouselets realized that the nest was actually a **Funny hat**!

"How can I help you?" asked the hat's wearer. She seemed to own the shop.

Nicky stepped forward. "Hello. We're looking for someone named **Kelly**."

The owner thoughtfully

tapped her chin. "Kelly? What's her last name?"

"Actually, we don't know," admitted Colette. "We only know her first name."

Suddenly, the boy with the blue skin POINTED behind the counter. On the center shelf were **three hats** stacked on top of one another. By themselves, they were nothing special, but when you put them all together, they looked just like the **tower** in Kelly's message!

All of the Thea Sisters recognized it.

"Excuse me," said Pam, trying to control her excitement. "Could we please see those THREE hats?"

"Of course! But may I ask why?" the woman asked in a slightly SUSPICIOUS tone.

"Because . . . um, they have a nice shape,"

Pam replied, thinking quickly.

The owner of the store nodded, but she seemed to be **STUDYING** the mouselets carefully now. She gave them the hats and they turned them around in their paws, not sure what they were looking for.

Nicky read the **TAG** inside one hat and noticed that the words sounded strange.

"Hey!" she called out. "Listen to this: 'Backward you can use me but not.' It sounds like part of a **clue**."

The Thea Sisters checked all three tags. When they read each one out loud, they found they could put them together to make a **riddle**.

"I run forward, never backward.
You can use me but not buy me.
Go where you can measure me!"

"It runs forward . . . you can use it . . . " Pam muttered, considering the clues.

"**It's time!**" Violet exclaimed. "It only goes forward, and you can use it but you cannot buy it."

"Brilliant!" said Nicky. "So where do we go where you can measure **time**?"

Violet turned to the owner. "Is there a clock shop near here?"

The woman seemed pleased. "The oldest **clock shop** in the city is just a few steps away." She wrote the **ADDRESS** on a piece of paper for Violet.

"Thank you," Violet said, but the shop owner had **DISAPPEARED** behind the counter.

A MATTER OF MINUTES

The Thea Sisters and the blue-skinned boy walked down the street and easily found the old CLOCK shop. A cast-iron sign with an hourglass on it hung above the door, squeaking as it moved in the breeze.

"This must be it!" Paulina said.

As they pushed open the door, they were greeted with a flood of noise. Dozens of clocks were marking time in unison, and the sound was incredible.

"what a fabumouse place!" Violet exclaimed.

TOCK
TOCK
TOCK TOCK TOCK TOCK
TICK TOCK TOCK TOCK

"You can say that again," agreed someone with a **DEEP** voice. It was the shop owner, an elderly rodent with a bushy white **mustache**. "These are the most precise clocks in the world! Each one is a jewel."

At that moment, the clocks all struck the hour. The sound was deafening!

Colette turned to the shop owner. "Excuse me, but we are looking for —"

"Oh, I know what you're looking for!" he interrupted her.

"**Really?**" asked the mouselets.

"But of course! You are looking for . . ." He paused as he ducked under the counter. Then he popped back up. "**This!**"

He held a wooden box in his paws.

"Oh, we're not here to shop," Violet said.

"Of course not! I have been holding this for you. They told me you would be coming to get it for **Miss Kelly**," the rodent replied.

The Thea Sisters exchanged glances. He knew Kelly! Violet took the **BOX**, and she saw the image of a **TOWER** carved on top.

"Who told you—" Paulina began, but the owner had already disappeared into the back room.

Violet opened the **BOX**. "There's a watch," she said. "It can tell both the hour and the date. **But it has stopped!**"

Colette studied the watch carefully. "Look, there's something engraved in it. It says 'eleven volte ninety-five.'"

"It must be another clue," Violet guessed.

Paulina frowned. "*Volte* means 'times' in Spanish. It sounds like a math lesson!"

"It's a **multiplication** problem!"

Nicky exclaimed. "Eleven times ninety-five. And the answer is . . . ONE THOUSAND FORTY-FIVE!"

"So what?" Paulina said, discouraged. "It's just a number. It could mean anything."

"Well, we're in a CLOCK shop, right?" Nicky said. "So maybe it's a time . . . ONE THOUSAND FORTY-FIVE could be 10:45!"

Paulina was excited again. "Let's move the hands of the watch to ten forty-five!"

They did, and nothing happened at first. Then the hands of the watch began to spin wildly. They landed on FOUR o'clock. The date in the little window read 3 FEBRERO —

which Paulina translated from Spanish as *February third*. Next to the date appeared a picture of a rose.

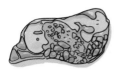

LET'S SPLIT UP!

The Thea Sisters were still confused.

"Let's review: We have a **time**, a **date**, and a rose," Nicky summed up as they left the store.

Violet studied the watch in her paw. "It could be some kind of meeting time."

"But today isn't the third of February!" Pam pointed out.

"And there are no roses around here," Colette said, LOOKING around.

Paulina stopped. "*Tres de febrero.* Roses. Hmm. Let me check something."

She typed on her MousePhone, calling up a website for tourists in Argentina.

"What are you looking for, a restaurant?" Pam asked hopefully. "I could eat!"

Paulina **s h o o k** her head. "No, I . . .

FOUND IT!"

They gathered around her screen.

"Tres de Febrero is a **PARK**!" Colette read in amazement.

"That's right," Paulina agreed. "I read about it. It's famouse for its rose garden!"

"Way to go!" Pam cheered. "So that means we need to be at this park at four o'clock. **WE'D BETTER GET MOVING!**"

The Thea Sisters followed the map on Paulina's phone and hurried to the park, trying to ignore how **tired** they were. The blue-skinned boy walked with them, gazing at all of the amazing city SIGHTS.

They reached the park in a half hour. They got a map from a young rodent wearing a

PARQUE TRES DE FEBRERO
sweatshirt. They had just
opened it to find the
location of the rose
garden when Colette
noticed something strange.

"Look, there is a symbol of
the tower STAMPED on
the map," she said, pointing.
"And under it is an image of a
WATER DROP!"

"It's like a special message
just for us," Pam realized. "Where's that
young rat who gave us this?"

They ran back to the park entrance, but
the young rat wasn't there. In his place was a
CHUBBY rodent with gray fur.

"Excuse me, but do you know where to
find the YOUNG rodent who was giving out

the maps?" Pam asked him.

He scowled. "What YOUNG rodent? I'm the only one who gives out maps!"

"**Cheese niblets!**" Paulina exclaimed, frustrated.

"Um, she means 'thanks,'" Colette said, grabbing her friend's arm. "Come on, let's explore the park!"

They walked back through the entrance and came to a covered **BRIDGE**. Across it, paths led to different areas of the park.

"Where are we going?" asked Paulina.

Colette studied the map. "I think this drop image is a clue, telling us to find **WATER**. But there's a lot of water in this park. There's a **lake** up ahead, but there are also drinking fountains, and a stream."

"But don't forget, a rose was part of the clue on the watch," Pam reminded them. "We might need to find the roses."

"Then there's nothing to do but SPLIT UP," Colette suggested.

Nicky nodded in agreement.

"I'll stay here and ftudy the map in case we missed anything," Violet said.

Everyone agreed on the plan. Violet sat on a bench with the map. Nicky ran around the park paths, looking for water. Pam and Colette headed to the rose garden. And Paulina and the blue-skinned boy explored the lake, where they found a pier with small boats for rent.

The boy's face lit up when he saw the boats. He had a huge fmile as he gazed across the lake's glassy surface.

I think this is the happiest he's been since he was shipwrecked! Paulina realized.

STRONGER
TOGETHER

While Paulina and the blue-skinned boy
EXPLORED the lake, Nicky ran along
the park paths. She saw mouselings playing
happily, and even passed eight fountains of
bubbling water — but she couldn't find any
clues around them.

I shouldn't have gone off **ALONE**, she thought. *I bet my friends could help me spot a clue!*

At the same time, Colette and Pam were **wandering** around the rose garden. Pam was **MUNCHING** on a triple-cheese sandwich she had purchased from a vendor.

"The garden hoses are **DRIPPING** water, but I don't see any clues," Colette said.

"Maybe we just can't spot them," Pam said.

"Let's see what the others think."

Colette and Pam went back to see Violet, who was still on the bench studying the **MAP**.

"We're not having any **LUCK**," Colette said.

"Maybe splitting up wasn't such a good idea," Pam admitted.

"I was thinking the same thing!" Violet said, *smiling*. "My Grandpa Chen used to say, 'If you want to move quickly, then go alone. But if you want to go far, you'll need company!'"

Nicky ran up and nodded to Colette and Pam. "Hey!" she cried, catching her breath. "You **came back**, too?"

"And so did we," said Paulina, walking up with the blue-skinned boy.

They were all together again!

Violet looked at her watch. "It's a quarter

till four, and we need to figure this out before four o'clock. Let's put our heads together and see what we can come up with!"

The THEA SISTERS gave a cheer:

"Let's do it!"

THE NINTH FOUNTAIN

Each THEA SISTER reported what she had **discovered**. Violet listened thoughtfully and looked at the map.

"So, Nicky, you said you found eight **FOUNTAINS**?" she asked.

Nicky nodded. "Yes, but no clues."

"Well, there are *nine* fountains on the map!" Violet said. "I think we should check it out."

Nicky **QUICKLY** marked off the eight fountains she had passed, so they knew which one to find. They hurried down the park paths until they came to a circular fountain. **CRYSTAL BURSTS** of water sprayed from its center.

Colette knelt down to examine the **YELLOW**

tiles that decorated the outside of the fountain.

"The design is lovely!" she said with appreciation. Then her blue eyes got wide. "LOOK! There's something here!"

Propped up against the bottom of the fountain was a **B O O K** with a worn-out silver cover. It was impossible to read the title, but poking out of the pages was a bookmark shaped like a TOWER!

The friends gathered around Colette, curious. The book seemed to be an old guidebook of Buenos Aires, written for tourists. On the marked page was information about an **old library**.

Colette read out loud. "The Library of Lost Worlds can be found at Calle del Sol, number seven. It holds a precious collection of rare volumes and ancient

manuscripts. The library is closed to the public and visits are allowed only for research or **INVESTIGATIONS**.'"

"Investigations . . . I would say that is exactly what we're doing!" Violet mused with a grin.

"Next stop: Calle del Sol!" Pam exclaimed. "But first . . . what do you say we investigate some of the Argentinian restaurants?"

The Thea Sisters burst out laughing. The boy with the blue skin smiled, taking in the good mood of his companions.

"Excellent idea, Pam," Nicky agreed. "We can't investigate on empty stomachs!"

LOST WORLDS

After a delicious meal, the friends went to number 7 Calle del Sol. They could make out the shape of a tower on the faded PLAQUE next to the front door.

"We're here!" Pam cried, ringing the bell. But no one answered. She rang again and again with no response.

Curious, Nicky SLOWLY turned the handle, and the heavy door opened with a creak. Everyone went inside to a dimly lit hallway.

The Library of Lost Worlds seemed DESERTED. Tall bookcases covered the walls, and every surface was covered with books.

Many volumes were

ancient, and some had precious silver and gold covers.

"How are we supposed to find a **clue** in all this?" Pam wondered, leaning against a stack of books.

KABOOM!

The books toppled over onto her!

"Pam, are you okay?" Paulina asked in alarm as the Thea Sisters ran to help their friend.

"I hope that my books are okay!" a deep voice ***THUNDERED***.

The mouselets turned around to find a tall rodent with brown fur.

"I am **FERNANDO TOWERS**, the librarian," the rodent said.

"Good morning," said Paulina respectfully. "We are—"

"I **know** who you are," he

interrupted. "I was waiting for you. Follow me."

Surprised, the group followed him down a narrow corridor that opened into a large circular room. Violet looked around at the titles of the books on the shelves; they were stories of ocean adventures, ancient marine MAPS, and texts about navigation and ocean animals.

Fernando gazed at them through his glasses. "I was curious to see if you would be able to solve my puzzles," he began.

"So it was you!" Pam exclaimed. "Why did you put us through all that?"

The librarian studied them carefully. "I know that you five have **stumbled upon** a mystery that no one seems to be able to solve." He nodded toward the **blue-skinned** boy.

"Yes," Violet responded. "All we know about our friend is that he was the victim of a **shipwreck** and he doesn't speak any known language. We tried communicating with **P I C T U R E S**, but we still don't know where he comes from."

Fernando nodded. "I would say you did the right thing by coming here," he said. "And, of course, Miss K. was very helpful."

"**Miss K.**?" asked Colette.

"Kelly," the librarian explained. "She gave you the first **CLUE** on your path to find me."

The mouselets looked at one another, **CONFUSED**.

"Perhaps I should explain. I am part of a **SECRET** group of experts who dedicate themselves to the study of MYSTERIOUS cases," he said, showing them a **silver-trimmed** card with a tower on it.

Institute of Incredible Stories

"The Institute of Incredible Stories? Where is that?" Nicky asked.

Fernando spun the GLOBE on the table and pointed to the southernmost continent.

"The I.I.S. is located in the most unexplored part of Earth: **Antarctica**," he replied. "Our scientists work there day and night to analyze cases that don't seem to have answers: TEXTS and codes that no rodent is able to decipher, evidence of **imaginary places** or mysterious creatures."

"Why have we never heard of it?" asked Paulina.

"We treat each case with the utmost **SECRECY**," Fernando explained. He paused, and his voice grew serious. "Some of the things we discover are too sensitive to be divulged to the **WORLD**. That is why it was so difficult to find me. I need to know that whoever is contacting me is worthy of my **TRUST**."

Nicky looked thoughtful. "So that means that the rodents who gave us the clues . . ."

". . . are all agents of the I.I.S.," the librarian finished for her. "They told me that you are united by a strong and selfless **friendship**. And you have proven that you sincerely want to **HELP** this stranger you have found."

He handed Paulina a card in the shape of a **TOWER**. "Take this pass to the I.I.S. It is valid for only **ONE** rodent. Tomorrow morning, one of you will meet me here at seven thirty to travel on to Antarctica. You must decide who will go. **GOOD LUCK!**"

GETTING READY

The THEA SISTERS checked in to the hotel and discussed who would go to **Antarctica**.

"It's too bad that we can't send *him*," Colette said, pointing to the blue-skinned boy. "Even though he is the **center** of this mystery, he wouldn't be able to **communicate**!"

"I nominate Paulina," said Nicky. "She was the one who **found** him on the beach at Whale Island."

The others immediately agreed, but Paulina was hesitant.

"Are you sure?" she asked nervously. "We've always done everything together!"

"Mr. Towers was very clear," Violet reminded her. "The pass is good for **JUST**

ONE rodent. You must go and tell them the story of our friend. It's our best bet!"

"It might be useful to bring along his **MEDALLION**," Colette suggested.

"I don't know if he would ever part with it!" Nicky pointed out.

Paulina opened her sketchbook. "Well, we can at least let him know what's happening."

She began to draw a **PICTURE** of herself saying good-bye to everyone and boarding a plane. He ɡᴇɴᴛʟʏ tapped her **paw** and stopped her before she could finish. Then he took the **MEDALLION** from

his neck and gave it to her, Smiling.

The Thea Sisters were stunned.

"He understood!" exclaimed Colette. She turned to him. "Do you understand us?"

The boy nodded, smiling. After all that time together, he had begun to understand a bit of their LANGUAGE.

Then he shocked them even more. He turned to Paulina, and in a melodious voice, he whispered, "Paulina."

The mouselets gasped with surprise.

"You—you can talk to us!"

Paulina cried happily.

They asked him to say more, but all he could manage was the name of his new friend. Even so, it was a good start!

ATLAS, THE PRINCE OF ATLANTIS

*W*ithout the medallion around his neck, the blue-skinned boy felt strange. He could still feel the weight of it pressing lightly against his chest. But when he went to touch it, he couldn't feel it anymore. Then he would remember—Paulina had it now.

Although he knew he was doing the right thing by lending it to her, he was breaking a promise. He had received the medallion when he took an oath, an ancient one that his ancestors had taken before him.

He would never forget that day—the most important day in his life. The ceremony took place in the Palace of the Ten Kings. He had knelt before the Great Master of Ceremonies as his family and the citizens of Atlantis looked on.

The Great Master had a long beard, and his braided hair touched the floor. "Today we entrust to you this medallion that opens the door to our beloved city," he had declared seriously. "Promise to honor it, defend it on your life, and never separate from it."

And the boy had replied in a sure voice, "I, Atlas, Prince of Atlantis, do promise. And I will keep this promise forever!"

And then the Great Master had placed the medallion around Atlas's neck. He heard his mother sniff back a happy tear, and when he stood up, he saw both his parents beaming with pride. They saw great things in him, and he did not want to let them down.

THE PALACE OF
THE TEN KINGS

Atlas was very young and inexperienced then. But he had never broken his oath. He knew his responsibility and was proud of it.

Now, however, something had changed. Despite the words that he had spoken in front of his whole kingdom, he had given the medallion to Paulina without thinking twice. Why had he done that?

The medallion needed to be protected, but it was also proof that the world he came from was real. And right now, it might be the only thing to save Atlantis from danger.

Atlas had never dreamed that by taking this journey he would put the land and people he loved at risk. In Atlantis, he had often dreamed of the marvelous world above the ocean. He believed that an encounter with this uncharted world would only bring good things to his people. Think of all the knowledge he could share with them!

Now, however, in his short time in the outside world, he had grown to understand that there were those who would harm Atlantis if they ever found it. They would misuse their discovery for their own gain.

All he could do was follow his instincts. Observing the five mouselets who took care of him, he knew that he could trust them. He felt closest to Paulina. She had kind eyes, and her face was so expressive that when he looked at her it was as if he could almost hear her thoughts. That is why he gave her the medallion. He knew that she would act only with the best intentions, and would help him find his way back home.

Without Paulina and her friends, he wouldn't have known what to do in this strange place. In Atlantis, he knew everyone, and everyone knew him. The map of the city was emblazoned in his mind, and he could get anywhere he needed to go very quickly. But in the outside world it took so long to get from one place to the next, and each place was different and surprising. And he still didn't fully understand the language, even if he had figured out a few words.

For those reasons, this world intimidated him and fascinated him at the same time. He wondered how his new friends would feel if they could travel to Atlantis. Surely they would think they were in some kind of dream, surrounded by so much beauty. He had tried to draw the golden and coral palaces, the bubbling fountains, and the lush gardens, but pencil strokes weren't enough to convey how amazing his home was.

Daily life in Atlantis was so different, too. How would he explain to his friends the job of the Teacher of Dreams? Or of the Crystal Sculptors?

Maybe, one day, when souls were moved only by a thirst for knowledge, the two worlds could meet. But right now, that day seemed far off.

Atlas sighed and looked out the window. Back home, when there was trouble, his mother would say, "The sky is blue for everyone." And here, Atlas thought, in this land called Argentina, the sky is blue for everyone, too.

EN ROUTE TO THE GLACIERS

The next **MORNING**, Paulina arrived at the Library of Lost Worlds at exactly **7:30**. She had on a small backpack, and wore around her neck the **precious** medallion that the boy had given her.

Fernando Towers was waiting in an **SUV** with muddy wheels.

"We're headed to the airport," he said. "This I.I.S. pass will allow you to **SKIP** lines

in the terminal."

He handed Paulina a kind of **PASSPORT** with the I.I.S. symbol on it. She climbed into the car and they took off through the city.

"Where are we flying?" Paulina asked.

"To Ushuaia, in the Argentinian province of **Tierra del Fuego**," the librarian replied. "It is almost two thousand miles from Buenos Aires and is the most southern city in the world. From there we will board a boat to Antarctica."

Paulina shivered with excitement. This was going to be an **AMAZING** adventure! She touched the **medallion**, thinking of the blue-skinned boy. She was determined to help her new **friend**!

As soon as she boarded the plane, the HECTIC pace of the last few days finally caught up with her. She dozed off and

dreamed of a beach with sparkling sand. The **BLUE-SKINNED** boy stood with her. He wore a splendid sea-silk tunic, and a crown GLITTERED on his head.

He opened his mouth to say something, but . . .

"Paulina! Paulina!"

Fernando Towers was shaking her right arm. "Wake up! The plane has landed!"

"Oh, it was just a *dream*," she murmured, opening her eyes. It had seemed so real!

Yawning, she followed the librarian off the plane and into the Ushuaia airport. A taxi waited to take them to the port, where they boarded a special **ice-breaking** ship.

"Now we will cross the Canal de Drake," Fernando explained. "It unites the **AtlanTIC** and **Pacific Oceans**. Often this bit of sea is very **turbulent**, but they predict calm waters today."

The ship pushed through the frozen waters for hours, until the Antarctica Peninsula

came into view. Paulina admired the giant ice **mountains** that rose from the water. They passed by **ice floes** inhabited by penguins and seals who watched the ship pass by, crushing **ice** in its wake.

"We'll be there soon; put these on," Fernando said, giving her a pair of **boots**.

"But I'm already wearing **BOOTS**," Paulina protested.

"Your boots are very fashionable, but these special ones will **protect** your paws from the **cold**," the librarian informed her. "The temperature is not expected to rise above **zero** degrees Fahrenheit while we're here. These boots help prevent **FROSTBITE** and have **SPECIAL** soles that will help you walk over snow and ice without slipping."

"Thank you!" Paulina said, and she quickly changed boots.

When they finally landed on the coast, she was glad to have them. Fernando Towers led the way through the **snowy** wilderness, and the boots helped her keep pace behind him.

Finally they came to a **wall of ice** that blocked their path.

"WE'RE HERE!" Fernando exclaimed. Then he stepped forward—and *DISAPPEARED* into the wall!

Surprised, Paulina followed him. The ice wall concealed a secret doorway! She stepped through and found herself in an **icy** cave. On the far wall, Fernando stood next to a tunnel dug into the ice.

"WELCOME TO THE GATES OF THE I.I.S.!" he cried.

THE INSTITUTE OF INCREDIBLE STORIES

Fernando Towers walked over to a small tower carved of ice and put the open palm of his right paw on top of it. A weak **HUMMING** sound began to spread throughout the cave. It grew stronger until a small orange shuttle emerged from the rear of the cave. The vehicle stopped in front of them and the transparent dome slowly lifted up.

"After you," Fernando said politely. Paulina hopped into the warm, padded passenger seat. The librarian got in and the dome sealed shut. Fernando steered the vehicle through the tunnel, and they entered the Antarctic underground.

Paulina looked through the dome in amazement at the icy walls, which were as smooth as glass and seemed to glow with a blue light from within.

The shuttle STOPPED in front of another wall of ice and Fernando got out. He pressed his paw against the ice wall, which lifted up, revealing a tall TOWER behind it: the TOWER whose image the Thea Sisters had been seeing in clues since their adventure began!

"A TOWER, here, beneath the ice?" Paulina asked in disbelief.

The librarian answered her with a cryptic smile. "Remember, 'The Tower's

Appearance is Deceiving'!" And with that, he took a few steps forward and disappeared.

Paulina was shocked, but then she realized the truth.

It's a hologram! she thought — an image **projected** into the air. She bravely took a few steps forward, and passed right **through** the tower's image.

"Welcome back, Mr. Theta! And I imagine you must be Paulina," a deep voice greeted her. A rodent with a **piercing** stare approached them.

"Paulina, this is **MR. ALPHA**, the founder of the I.I.S.," Fernando said.

"Um, hello," Paulina said, a little bit nervously.

"I've heard that you have an **INTERESTING** case for us," Mr. Alpha said.

She nodded and reached for the medallion, but Mr. Alpha held up a paw to **STOP** her.

"Before you tell me your story, I would like to **SHOW** you the institute. There is also someone you should meet," he said, and Paulina followed him.

Mr. Alpha led Paulina through the busy corridors of the I.I.S. She noticed that every room had a door of a different **color**.

They stopped at a **purple door** first. Mr. Alpha pressed his paw on it and it slid open. They stepped into a room with purple walls and a sign that said Non-Classified Material.

"Right now we are working on a **fascinating** breakthrough," he told her, approaching an area of lab tables covered with **TEST TUBES** and microscopes.

He pointed to a sealed glass cylinder. "It's an amazing metal," he explained. "It can change from a GAS to a liquid to a SOLID with no catalyst! Quite remarkable."

Inside the cylinder, Paulina watched as a silver liquid took on the shape of a cube, and then suddenly vaporized before her eyes.

Next, they went into a room with a GREEN DOOR, with a sign that said BOTANIC AREA.

"In here, we are studying a plant that has incredible properties of language," Mr. Alpha said proudly.

An enormous and thriving plant grew in the center of the room. Small orange fruits shaped like teardrops hung from its branches.

"If you eat the fruit, you are able to COMMUNICATE with other species of animals," Mr. Alpha explained.

Paulina wasn't sure if she had heard right, but Mr. Alpha quickly led her to a small pool dug into the ice. Several **PENGUINS** swam happily in the water. A researcher was talking in a STRANGE language to one of the penguins—and the bird seemed to be **talking** back!

"Amazing!" murmured Paulina.

"It certainly is," Mr. Alpha agreed.

He led her to a **BLUE DOOR**. "This is the area that is dedicated to **MAPPING UNKNOWN TERRITORIES**," he explained.

He opened the door, and Paulina's eyes widened at the sight of the framed maps and **ancient** manuscripts that covered the walls. The room was a researcher's dream!

"This is our collection of *maps* from unknown places, as well as accounts of trips to uncharted lands," Mr. Alpha told her.

In the corner of the room, a researcher stood studying at a table. Her blond fur was piled on top of her head. Mr. Alpha tapped her on the shoulder and she looked up.

"Let me introduce

you to **Miss Kappa**," he said. "She is our top archaeologist and an expert in mysterious finds. She will be the one working with you on your **case**."

The rodent met Paulina with a friendly smile, and shook her paw.

"Welcome!" she said.

Paulina immediately felt close to her, and realized who she must be. "Miss Kappa! So you are—"

"Kelly Parker, Thea Stilton's **friend**," the researcher finished for her. "My code name here at the institute is Miss Kappa. I am so **happy** to be able to help you. Thea has told me all about you and your friends. She said that you are all **VERY SMART**, and I understand you have stumbled upon a very INTERESTING case. Why don't you tell me everything from the beginning?"

CROSSED MESSAGES

That **NIGHT**, Paulina settled into the room reserved for guests of the I.I.S. She had seen so many amazing things that day! She was exhausted, but she wanted to let her **friends** know what was happening.

Earlier, one of the I.I.S. staff had helped 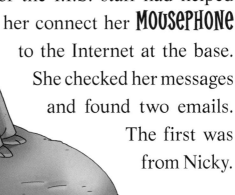 her connect her **MOUSEPHONE** to the Internet at the base. She checked her messages and found two emails. The first was from Nicky.

From: Nicky
To: Paulina
Subject: News from Buenos Aires

Dear Pauly,

How are you? How was your trip? What is Antarctica like? It must be a marvelous place. I've always dreamed of going!

There's nothing really new here. Our friend with the blue skin is getting weaker and weaker, so we let him rest and try to keep him calm.

There is good news, however: He's making progress learning the language. We were finally able to get him to say his name: Atlas! Isn't that a beautiful name? Plus, he drew a picture. I'm attaching a scanned copy of it. We weren't able to understand what it's about, but maybe you can figure it out. When you can, please send us an email!

All of us send you big hugs! We are so proud of you! Talk to you soon.

Yours,
Nicky

Paulina studied the **picture**.

"That object next to him looks like a crown," she murmured to herself. "Just like the one he was wearing in my dream! But how could that be? And that circle design is the same one that's on the MEDALLION."

Lost in thought, Paulina opened up the second email. It was the message that I had sent to all of the Thea Sisters.

From: Thea
To: Paulina, Colette, Violet, Pam, Nicky
Subject: News from Mouseford

Dearest Thea Sisters,

I hope that you and the boy with the blue skin are all well and safe.

Unfortunately, I have some bad news: Professor Quasar has disappeared from Mouseford without a trace. Even his assistant seems to have vanished.

I did some investigating, and I am certain that Quasar's interest in our friend is based on greed and not science. I am afraid he has left in search of you!

I've decided that the best way for me to help you now is to leave Whale Island and return home. I'm going to search my archives to see if I can find anything that might help you solve this mystery. I've done years of research on all kinds of strange things!

Keep me updated on any news, and please be careful.

A big hug,
Thea

Paulina **typed** a response to everyone.

From: Paulina
To: Thea, Colette, Violet, Pam, Nicky
Subject: Re: News from Mouseford

Dear Thea and Thea Sisters,

After a long trip, I arrived at the magnificent I.I.S. headquarters. I had the chance to tour the entire building, and you would not believe the incredible things I saw! I wasn't allowed to take photos, but I promise to tell you all about it when I get back.

I also met the head of the I.I.S., Mr. Alpha, who is very interested in Atlas's story. He introduced me to the researcher who will be working on our case: Her code name is Miss Kappa, but she's really Kelly Parker, Thea's friend! She seemed really nice. She promised me that tomorrow we would analyze the case together and decide what to do.

I miss you guys a lot! I will email you tomorrow and let you know how things are going.

Yours,
Paulina

She then **Hit** SEND, but the email never reached me or her friends. Paulina was allowed to *receive* emails at the I.I.S., but she didn't realize that no communication could *leave* the **TOP SECRET** facility unless it was cleared by the security team. For now, her communication would have to wait.

VANISHED CONTINENTS

The next morning, Paulina heard a **knock** on the door of her room. It was Kelly! She greeted Paulina with a big smile.

"Good morning! Are you up yet? I would like to look at the **MEDALLION** you told me about," she said eagerly.

Paulina removed it from around her neck and gave it to the scientist, who studied it in her paws. Her eyes seemed to **light** up.

"This could be the **REAL** thing," she murmured.

"Do you know what it means?" Paulina asked, **anxious** for some answers.

"Maybe," Kelly replied. "But I need to

check something out. Come with me!"

The two of them walked into a room marked **Vanished Continents**. More **MAPS** covered the walls here, too, but the shapes of the countries were unfamiliar.

Kelly went right to a computer with a large **screen** in the center of the room. She carefully placed the **MEDALLION** on a scanner and pressed a button. A 3-D image of the medallion appeared on the screen, along with what looked like technical data.

"The computer doesn't recognize the **metal** that the medallion is made of," Kelly said, analyzing the results. "But it has identified the **SYMBOL** on the back!"

She moved to the wall with maps and pointed to a **ripped** map with *burned* edges. It showed what looked like an island. The legend on the map read: **Atlantis**.

In the center of the island was the same **SYMBOL** that appeared on the medallion.

"This map shows the legendary kingdom of **Atlantis**, and this symbol represents the capital city," Kelly explained. "It was first described by the ancient Greek philosopher Plato. He wrote that Atlantis was an island that was home to an ENLIGHTENED civilization. Some believe that the island mysteriously **sank** thousands of years ago."

She held the **MEDALLION** next to the symbol on the map. There was no doubt about it — they were **EXACTLY** the same!

"The I.I.S. archives contain information

ATLANTIS—VANISHED CONTINENT

Described in legends and stories, Atlantis is home to a thriving civilization with advanced technology. Writers have told of a vast, rich land, filled with unusual plants and precious metals. The most widespread metal is orichalcum, a mysterious fire-colored material. The reasons why this magnificent island disappeared remain unknown.

According to the Greek philosopher Plato, the capital city of Atlantis is made up of alternating concentric circles of land and sea.

Where is this lost continent located? Hypotheses about this abound. Many believe that the island lies in the center of either the Atlantic Ocean or the Mediterranean Sea, deep below the waves. Others believe that Atlantis can be found in North Africa, buried under the drifting sands of the Sahara Desert. But no definite evidence of it has been found in any suspected locations.

about many **vanished** civilizations," Kelly went on. She went back to the computer and started to type. "Let's see what we can find."

The Atlantis page **POPPED UP**, and she and Paulina read it together.

Paulina was stunned. "Based on this, it makes me think that our friend . . ."

". . . could come from **Atlantis**," concluded Kelly.

Paulina tried to put the pieces of the puzzle together. "The **BLUE SKIN** . . . his strange language . . ."

"These are important **clues**," Kelly said with a nod. "He could be a descendant of the ancient people of Atlantis."

"Then there's the metal that the **MEDALLION** is made of," Paulina said, studying the screen. "It certainly sounds like this **ORICHALCUM**."

"I agree," Kelly said. She scrolled down

the page to read more. After a moment, she pointed at the screen. "Look! It says here that the symbol of CIRCLES, the one that looks like a bird's-eye view of the capital of Atlantis, is a *royal* symbol."

"Royal?" Paulina asked in disbelief.

Kelly's blue eyes SHINED with excitement. "Yes, Paulina. I believe that this is the **king's** medallion!"

It was almost impossible to believe. Paulina spoke slowly. "That means that Atlas is . . ."

". . . a king. Or maybe a PRINCE," Kelly guessed.

Paulina couldn't wait to tell her friends. The strange boy who had washed ashore, the one who had become their friend, might be a real live PRINCE!

A SUSPICIOUS CHARACTER

Back in Buenos Aires, Violet and Nicky were returning to their hotel after a trip to the grocery store.

"I hope we **hear** from Paulina soon," Violet said worriedly.

Inside the hotel lobby, a bizarre rodent was at the reception desk. He was a short mouse wearing a long COAT, a hat, and sunglasses. As they passed by, they heard him say, "Yes, I am looking for five mouselets."

"He's talking about us!" Violet said.

Nicky signaled for her to keep quiet and pulled her behind a column in the lobby. Now they could listen without being seen.

"What do you mean, who am I?" the

rodent was protesting. "I'm . . .
um . . . their **uncle**!"

Nicky took a quick **PHoto** of
the rat with her MousePhone.

"Let's go to our room," she
whispered to Violet. "I have a
bad feeling about this."

recognized the face immediately.

"**Quasar!**" she cried.

Kelly leaned over to look at the photo, and exclaimed, "**MR. Beta!**"

The two stared at each other. "**How do you know him?**" they asked in unison.

Paulina went first. "Quasar showed up at Mouseford and said he was a marine biology researcher," she explained. "But we suspect that he wants to **KIDNAP** Atlas!"

"Quasar," Kelly said, shaking her head. "So that's what he's calling himself now! His code name at the I.I.S. was Mr. Beta, and he was one of our most **brilliant** scientists."

Kelly looked **thoughtful** for a while, then she nodded to Paulina.

"Follow me. I want to show you something."

They went to a hallway full of framed **photographs**. Kelly stopped in front of a photo recognized the face immediately.

"**Quasar!**" she cried.

Kelly leaned over to look at the photo, and exclaimed, "**MR. Beta!**"

The two stared at each other. "**How do you know him?**" they asked in unison.

Paulina went first. "Quasar showed up at Mouseford and said he was a marine biology researcher," she explained. "But we suspect that he wants to **KIDNAP** Atlas!"

"Quasar," Kelly said, shaking her head. "So that's what he's calling himself now! His code name at the I.I.S. was Mr. Beta, and he was one of our most **brilliant** scientists."

Kelly looked **thoughtful** for a while, then she nodded to Paulina.

"Follow me. I want to show you something."

They went to a hallway full of framed **photographs**. Kelly stopped in front of a photo

"It's worth a try," Nicky said. "But what should we do in the meantime? That **strange rodent** is after us!"

Luckily, just minutes before, Paulina had received clearance to send messages from I.I.S. headquarters. She and Kelly were doing more **RESEARCH** on Atlantis.

"A MESSAGE!" she said when she heard her phone beep. But her face **saddened** when she read it.

"Bad news?" Kelly asked.

"There's a **suspicious** rodent at my friends' hotel in Buenos Aires," Paulina explained. "They sent me a **photo** and asked if I would work on clearing up the image."

Paulina pressed a button on her phone and the **special** application went to work. It cleared up the blurriness and removed the hat and glasses from the rodent. Paulina

rodent was protesting. "I'm . . .
um . . . their uncle!"

Nicky took a quick PHoto of
the rat with her MousePhone.

"Let's go to our room," she
whispered to Violet. "I have a
bad feeling about this."

When they got to the room, Colette and Pam immediately noticed the troubled looks on their friends' faces.

"What's wrong?" asked Pam.

Nicky and Paulina quickly explained about the **suspicious** character in the lobby. Nicky showed them the photo.

"It's not a great picture," she admitted. "And the whole thing is a little ***BLURRY***. But he seems familiar, doesn't he?"

Pam smacked her forehead with her paw. "Of course! Paulina!"

"What about her?" Nicky asked.

"She has a program on her MousePhone that can **CLEAN UP** photos," Pam said. "It's pretty amazing. It can remove layers from the image so you see what's underneath. Let's try to send her the picture of this guy!"

of two researchers in white coats.

"IT'S HIM!" exclaimed Paulina.

"Exactly," said **Kelly**. "The tall rodent next to him is Mr. Alpha. Years ago, they were **best friends** and always worked together. Then Mr. Beta **RAN OFF** with the results of extremely important research that he and Mr. Alpha had worked on together for months. The I.I.S. lost faith in him, but we have kept track of him. He travels the world, seeking **mysterious** cases that he can exploit for his own personal gain."

"So that's why he's so interested in **Atlas**," Paulina realized. "We've got to warn my friends immediately. They're in **DANGER**!"

ESCAPE FROM BUENOS AIRES

"It's Paulina!" Nicky cried a moment later, when her friend's message reached her.

"She's finally written back!" cheered Pam.

"What does she say?" asked Violet.

Nicky read the message out loud. "'The mouse you photographed is Quasar, and he wants to capture Atlas. You need to leave the city immediately. Go back to the library and ask Pablo for help.'"

"Cheesecake!" Pam exclaimed. "How did Quasar manage to follow us here?"

"I don't know, Pam," Colette replied. "But I think we need to do what Paulina says. Let's HURRY!"

The friends looked at one another. "But

who is Pablo?" they asked in unison.

Then they heard heavy footsteps in the hallway. Someone was approaching their room.

"I bet it's Quasar. QUICK!" Nicky said, opening the French doors that led to the FIRE ESCAPE. "We can climb down."

Colette leaned out the window and saw how far up they were from the ground.

"This doesn't seem like such a good idea," she said nervously. "Those metal stairs look dangerous, and we'd have to leave our luggage behind, and—"

Before she could say anything more, they all heard the sound of someone trying to force open the lock on the door.

"He's trying to get in. Let's go!" Violet urged, taking Colette by the paw and leading her onto the fire-escape landing.

Pam and Atlas **QUICKLY** followed behind. Nicky tossed some items into a backpack and climbed down after them.

They stopped a **taxi** as soon as they reached the street.

"To Calle del Sol, number seven!" Violet said, and the driver **took off** for the library.

At that moment, back at the I.I.S. building, Paulina and Kelly were heading back to the **icy** surface. They had gone to Mr. Alpha and Mr. Theta, the librarian, and told them everything. Together, they had **discussed** what should be done.

"Mr. Beta, or rather, Quasar, never moves without a **strong** motive," said Mr. Theta. "He is most certainly **up to no good**. We need to protect Atlas and get him to a safe place."

Mr. Alpha nodded in agreement. "Kelly,

you and Paulina must **return** to Argentina to help your friends," said the director. "But Buenos Aires is no longer safe. You must all travel to another city in Argentina: Iguazú. Alert Pablo!"

"Will do," Kelly assured them. "We'll move right away!"

The two mice raced out of the institute. Paulina was frightened for her friends, but **excited** at the same time. She couldn't wait to see them and **Atlas** again.

"Now that I know his name and where he's from, maybe we can **COMMUNICATE** better," she said hopefully as the ship brought her and Kelly back through the

frozen sea to Ushuaia.

"There's a reason we're going to Iguazú," Kelly informed her. "There is an I.I.S. lab there that specializes in the study of lost **languages**. The linguists there have been able to decipher some very difficult ancient languages. I believe that they might be able to **UNDERSTAND** Atlas."

Paulina was even more excited.

"Now we can find out if he's really **THE PRINCE OF ATLANTIS!**"

AN UNEXPECTED
DEPARTURE

The Thea Sisters and Atlas hurried out of the taxi as soon as it pulled up in front of the **Library of Lost Worlds**. Pam reached the door first and headed inside. A young rodent was stocking the shelves with **BOOKS**.

He turned around as they came inside

"Hey!" said Nicky. "You're the one who gave us the **map** in the park!"

The young mouse smiled. "Hi, nice to meet you. I'm **Pablo**."

"So you're the one we're supposed to see," Nicky said.

Pablo nodded. "Yes. Are you ready to **GO**?"

"Go where?" the Thea Sisters asked.

"You'll find out when we get there," he

replied **mysteriously**. "We've got to hurry—a plane is waiting for us."

The friends trusted Pablo, so they took a taxi with him to a small airport, where they boarded a **tiny plane**.

"Um, how long is our flight, exactly?" Nicky asked nervously. The idea of being cooped up in such a small craft made her uneasy.

"It's a short trip," Pablo **promised**.

"Are you sure no one will be able to follow us?" Violet asked, thinking of Quasar.

"I've already thought of that," Pablo said. "We're going to take a boat down the *RIVER* for the last leg of our trip."

A few hours later they landed near the Iguazú River in northern ARGENTINA. When they got out, Pablo led them on a path

through the forest. When they reached the river, they boarded a **rubber** raft. They floated down the river **peacefully**, accompanied by

the chirping of birds. Then a deafening roar filled their ears.

"It almost sounds like a —" Violet began . . . and then she saw it.

"WATERFALL!" the Thea Sisters cried.

They had entered a cove surrounded by some of the biggest waterfalls they had ever seen!

"We're here!" Pablo announced as they watched the cascading water in amazement.

He steered the raft toward a small beach and pointed to a helicopter that was descending in front of the waterfalls.

"There are Miss Kappa and your friend," he told them. "After we meet up with them, we'll go to the SECRET BASE!"

ATLAS SPEAKS

The reunion of Paulina and the rest of the THEA SISTERS was full of hugs, but too rushed for them to catch up. Kelly opened a bag and produced full rainsuits for all of them. Then they all boarded the raft, and Pablo steered it right toward one of the WATERFALLS!

"WATCH OUT!" Violet yelled. "We're going right into the water!"

"Don't be scared," Pablo responded with a smile. "I know the way."

To the amazement of the Thea Sisters, he skillfully steered the raft UNDER the waterfall, to the dry space between the stream of water and the rocky wall.

"How marvelous!" Nicky exclaimed.

Next, Pablo steered them through a **SECRET PASSAGE** in the rock wall, and they were suddenly surrounded by DARKNESS. Violet gave a frightened gasp, and Pam reached out and took her friend's paw. A ray of light soon lit up the passage and Pablo docked next to a stone platform. Everyone got off the raft and took off their RAIN GEAR.

Kelly led them to a smooth spot on the rock wall and pressed her paw on it. A SECRET door slid open.

"We're here!" she announced.

They followed her into an enormouse room full of **electronic** equipment. Kelly confidently marched to a **MACHINE** that had two seats with a clear helmet above each one. The posts holding up the helmets were attached to a large computer MONITOR, and

a green wire connected the two helmets.

"Let's see what we can do!" Kelly exclaimed.

She told Atlas to sit in one seat and Paulina to sit in the other. Then she lowered a **helmet** onto each one's head and switched on the machine. A **BLUE LIGHT** shined from the monitor and bounced off the ceiling. Kelly motioned for Atlas to say something. His **musical** voice filled the room.

To everyone else, it sounded **STRANGE**. But not to Paulina. With the helmet on, she could **clearly** understand, as if Atlas were speaking in her language.

"Do you understand what I'm saying?" Atlas asked her.

Paulina shivered with excitement. It was so amazing to be able to communicate with her friend at last!

"Yes," she replied in a **shaky** voice.

"So when I say thank you for saving my life, you understand me?" Atlas asked.

Paulina felt **TEARS** come to her eyes. **"Yes!"**

The others watched in amazement; it looked like Paulina and Atlas could communicate! Atlas began to tell his story, and Paulina repeated his tale for them.

THE STORY OF PRINCE ATLAS

You already know my name—Atlas—and I already know your names. Without you all, I wouldn't be alive. So I shall tell you a story that I swore I would never tell anyone. But over these days, I have come to know you, and I trust you all.

I come from a faraway land that sits deep in the ocean: Atlantis. I am the prince of Atlantis. My father is the king, and I will take his throne one day. It is a happy and peaceful kingdom, with a

history thousands of years old.

Legend has it that many centuries ago, our kingdom was on the surface of the water. On this lush island, my ancestors developed advanced technology and possessed great knowledge that allowed them to live peacefully. Everyone prospered.

One day, however, all of this changed, and the waters of the sea swallowed our island. Much of it was destroyed, but the capital city, home to all of our most important buildings, was unharmed and sank to the bottom of the sea.

Great crystal domes protected the capital city and the buildings, plants, animals, and people that lived inside. The domes kept the air in and kept the dangerous sea waters out.

Our engineers found a way to bring down light to our ocean depths so our plants could survive. The life cycle continued. The people got used to life in the underwater city, and over time, forgot the outside world.

Paulina couldn't believe the story she was hearing. It was incredible!

"Ask him if he knows what caused the disaster," suggested Kelly.

Paulina asked, but Atlas shook his head.

My people tell many legends of what caused the catastrophe. Some say it was an earthquake or a comet. But only my father knows the secret truth. Every king learns the history on the day of his coronation, and he solemnly swears never to tell.

"And to think that here on the surface, we

don't believe you exist," Kelly murmured.

Paulina translated and the prince **SMiLED**.

It is the same with us. In Atlantis, no one really believes that a world exists above the sea. Instead, many believe that it never existed. My people think that there has never been another civilization besides our own.

Everyone was ***silent*** for a moment. Then Violet spoke up.

"Paulina, can you ask him how he washed up on the **beach**?" she asked.

Atlas let out a sigh when he heard Paulina repeat the question.

I didn't believe that the outside world was a legend. I even had some proof.

"What kind of proof?" Paulina asked.

In the royal library there are ancient books that describe your world, but everyone thinks they are myths, or legends to be told

*to children. In fact, my sister and I heard
them when we were young.*

"You have a **SiSTER**?" Paulina asked.

Atlas smiled tenderly and nodded.

*Astra. We both heard the stories, and I
felt that they were too detailed to have been
made up. Growing up, my desire to uncover
the truth behind the legends grew stronger
and stronger. I dreamed about leaving the
kingdom and going exploring, but . . .*

His voice trailed off. Everyone held their
breath, waiting to hear the rest. Atlas closed
his eyes for a moment, and then his
melodious voice filled the room once again.

*I am the heir to the throne. It is my duty to
take care of my people. I never should have
left them.*

Paulina's voice **trembled** with emotion as she repeated Atlas's **extraordinary** confession to the others.

My father didn't understand my desire to travel. He called me a dreamer and reminded me of my obligations to my people. So I resigned myself to staying in my kingdom, and I buried my dreams deep within my heart.

Colette GASPED and grabbed Pam's paw. How tragic!

The years passed, until my father decided it was time to hand me his throne. Although I was young, he was tired of ruling. I was not happy with this decision, but I knew that I must obey him and accept my destiny. Then something happened—something I never expected. . . .

Atlas stopped. For an instant, he seemed

lost in thought. Then he continued.

A few days before my coronation, I met my father in the throne room. I was prepared to tell him that I would give up my dreams and become king. I thought he would take my words as a sign of maturity.

But he stopped me from speaking and led me to a room in our palace that I had never seen before. He said to me, "My son, to be a true king you must love, above all, the people in your kingdom. But you have a different love in your heart—a love of adventure. Until you slake this thirst, you will never be a good leader. So I give you my permission to leave and follow your dreams."

Then he showed me an amazing watercraft made of metal and pearl. He told me that in this vehicle I could leave Atlantis and travel

to the surface.

The Thea Sisters were **transfixed** by the story. "So you left," Colette murmured.

Yes. Leaving Atlantis and my loved ones was not easy, but I knew it was the right thing to do.

The prince smiled and his eyes sparkled as he remembered the excitement he felt. But his expression turned sad.

Just as I was about to leave, my mother began to cry, worried about what might happen to me. I had no idea what my future held, and it scared me a little. But more than anything, I wanted to explore, and that feeling was stronger than my fear. This was my only chance to make my dream come true—the dream I had held in my heart for so long. I assured my mother that I would return and become the king she raised me to

be. Then I got in the ship and never looked back.

"And what happened next?" Paulina asked.

At first, the trip was smooth. The ship rode the currents, rising higher and higher through miles of water.

I had only a vague idea of where to go, but I trusted that sooner or later I would reach the surface of the sea. I had food and instruments with me, and a book that I had discovered on the shelves of the royal library. It was a travel diary, and on the very first page was a map that showed Atlantis linked to another continent! I know the map could have come from the writer's imagination, but I had a feeling that it was real. The author's name was Antonio

Voyager. He was a citizen of Atlantis, but he said that he was born in a city far, far away—"Lisbon."

"**Lisbon**?" Pam exclaimed in disbelief.

"Lisbon isn't a legendary city," Violet said. "It's the capital of Portugal!"

Atlas began to nod **energetically** when he heard the translation.

Yes! I have never heard of this Portugal, but it is obviously a real place. Which means that Voyager's story was real, too.

Using Voyager's map, I traveled far away from my kingdom. The water gradually changed color. Finally, I reached the surface. An explosion of light came over me, and I was astonished. I could see the sky and clouds for the very first time! It was amazing.

I sailed around for several hours, letting

the waves carry me. Then night fell, and with the darkness came a terrible wind. The sea began to churn violently.

"**THE STORM!**" Paulina realized.

Then dazzling lights appeared in the sky, accompanied by loud booming noises. The waves swirled around my ship. I fell into the water and began to sink, as if the water wanted me back in its depths. Luckily, a dolphin came to my rescue, and I grabbed his fin before I passed out.

The prince **gazed** at Paulina.

When I opened my eyes again, I saw you.

THE BLUE CURRENT

Kelly was stunned by Atlas's story. She had spent many years at the **I.I.S.** researching the kingdom of Atlantis. She had longed to find PROOF that it existed, and to pinpoint its location. But she had never succeeded.

Yet now, right in front of her, was living, breathing proof of the lost civilization! Stories of Atlantis had thrilled researchers all over the world for centuries. She knew they would love to be in her shoes right now.

But when Pablo had suggested that they immediately let people know about their discovery, she responded firmly, "No, Pablo, it would be too **DANGEROUS**. We need to protect Atlas and his kingdom from those who would harm it."

She was ~~thinking~~, of course, of Mr. Beta—Professor Quasar. She shuddered to think that he might have kidnapped Atlas. Many stories talked about the precious metals and jewels in Atlantis. She knew a greedy rodent like Mr. Beta would do anything to get his paws on them.

Atlas still had more to say, so Paulina translated for him.

I am so thankful to all of you for taking care of me. I couldn't have survived here without your help. I've felt very weak ever since I set foot on land, and it is difficult for me to think. I believe that, after so many centuries under the sea, the inhabitants of Atlantis would have a hard time living in the outside world. The climate is a strain on us.

"So what do you want to do?" Paulina

asked. "We want to **HELP** you."

Atlas was thoughtful for a while.

I would like to go back home. I want to see my parents and my sister again.

"Do you know how to get back?"

He shook his head.

I lost my ship in the storm. And even if I did have the ship, I'm not sure if I could map my journey home. I need to find the Blue Current.

Antonio Voyager

"The Blue Current?" Paulina asked.

Antonio Voyager called it — or rather, them — that. He wrote that there are several Blue Currents that run under the ocean's surface. They cannot always be found, but when they are, they connect the surface to Atlantis. I followed one of these currents to the surface. Antonio Voyager described them correctly in his diary.

"But Antonio's diary . . ." Paulina murmured apprehensively.

Was lost in the storm, with all of my things, confirmed Atlas, shaking his head.

"I'm curious. What happened to Antonio Voyager?" Colette asked. "He said he was born in **LISBON**, yet he lived in Atlantis. How did his life end?"

No one knows for sure. Life in Atlantis made Voyager restless. His health was not very good, and he kept remembering Lisbon as a marvelous place.

"So he wanted to return home," Paulina guessed.

On the very last page of the diary, he says that he longed to return to Lisbon. He seemed ready to leave. I don't know how or when he left Atlantis, but I do remember how the diary ends: with a picture of a tower.

Everyone turned to look at Kelly, who shook her head. "I don't know anything about an I.I.S. **CONNECTION** to Voyager. The **TOWER** symbol might just be a coincidence."

There was a word under the tower, Atlas

said. *I don't know if it was written in your language, but the word was* Belém.

"*Belém*?" Paulina repeated.

The Thea Sisters all looked at Violet, who was usually a walking **encyclopedia**.

"In fact," Violet said, "there is a tower in Lisbon with that name. It was constructed by a king who supported **explorations** by land and sea."

Atlas's eyes lit up with hope.

So if Voyager was able to return home, he might have brought with him information about his trip!

"And if he didn't?" asked Violet.

Then there would be no way for me to find the Blue Currents and go home, Atlas said.

Pam did not like seeing **Atlas** look so sad. "Of course Voyager got home!" she said confidently. "And now we've got to follow his **tracks**!"

"Pam's right," agreed Paulina. "From what you've told us, it sounds like Antonio Voyager was a **clever** explorer. So I'm sure he found a way to return **home**."

"We should go to Lisbon and see if Voyager left anything behind," Nicky suggested.

Violet looked thoughtful. "We should also contact Thea. I believe she was studying **MARINE CURRENTS** during her trip on whale migration. Maybe she can help us."

Kelly **DISCONNECTED** the translation **machine**. "So we have a plan! Pablo will take you to the airport and get you on a plane to **Lisbon**. I will return to the I.I.S. and see what I can do from there."

"**Perfect!**" agreed Paulina, although

she was a little bit sad. She would miss using the machine to talk to Atlas.

The Thea Sisters gave a cheer.

"LET'S GO! LISBON AWAITS!"

LISBON, HERE WE COME!

Before they left for Portugal, the Thea Sisters contacted me and I sent them some **information** about the city and Belém Tower. Violet read the information out loud on the flight.

"'Lisbon, the capital of Portugal, is a hilly city that overlooks the Rio Tejo. Many sailors and **explorers** departed from the city's historic port to search for far-off lands.'"

"Just like Antonio Voyager!" Colette interrupted. "He was an explorer!"

Violet nodded. "The sea's presence can be felt in the BREEZE that caresses the streets of the city, and it is seen in the blue of the azulejos, the glazed ceramic designs that decorate the buildings there."

"**BLUE!**" Atlas exclaimed, recognizing the word.

"Does it say anything about **BELÉM TOWER**?" Nicky asked impatiently.

"Let's see," Violet said, scanning the pages. "Here it is. The Belém Tower was finished in the early 1500s. It was used for defense and is also considered a **gateway** to the city. It

is located on a tiny island at the mouth of the RIO TEJO. Visitors there can CLIMB up the tower."

Violet showed her friends a photo of the tower and the directions I had provided.

"Perfect! We'll go right there!" Paulina said.

"And what happens when we get there?" Pam asked. "What are we looking for?"

"I don't know," Paulina admitted. "A **CLUE**, I guess. Anything that Voyager might have left behind."

"Is there anything about him in Thea's report?" asked Nicky.

Violet shook her head. "Apparently, his name isn't in any history book. I just hope that he really **exi∫ted**!"

"Of course he did!" Colette said **confidently**. She nodded to Atlas, who was looking at **clouds** through the window. There was no sense in upsetting their friend.

At that moment, Pam's stomach growled.

"Does Thea say anything about **food** in there?" Pam asked.

"She wrote a whole chapter about it, called 'Notes for Pam,'" Violet joked. "But seriously, she does say that Belém is known for its **pastry shops**. They're famous for a treat called *pastel de Belém*, which is a sort of **vanilla custard tart**."

"Sounds delicious!" Nicky exclaimed. "As soon as we arrive, let's go get a **snack**!"

They landed in the Lisbon airport a few hours later. After checking in at their hotel, they decided to **explore** the city. Following my directions, they boarded a **TRAM** and rode **UP AND DOWN** the hilly streets of the city's historic district.

The tree-lined streets, old buildings, and quaint cafés *CHARMED* the mouselings. When they reached the Rio Tejo, Nicky cried

out, "Look over there! It's **amazing**!"

An imposing FORT with gray stone towers overlooked the riverbank.

"That is St. George's Castle," Violet explained.

Then the tram began to travel along the river. Atlas and the THEA SISTERS were so enthralled with the **beauty** of the landscape that they almost didn't realize they had reached Belém. When they got off the tram, they headed to the nearest pastry shop for some DELICIOUS tarts. As they ate, they discussed their plan.

"The first thing to do is find out if Voyager ever returned to Lisbon," Violet said.

"And then see if he left any **clues**," added Nicky.

"Then I think we should start at BELÉM TOWER, right?" Colette asked.

Pam licked the last bit of custard from her paw and stood up.

"To the tower!" she cried.

BELÉM TOWER

The *majestic* Belém Tower stood just off the bank of the Rio Tejo, separated by a narrow canal of water.

"What a beautiful building!" commented Colette, admiring the **stone** balconies and the **decorations** on its walls.

Atlas, meanwhile, was already headed down the walkway that led to the tower entrance. He was impatient to discover if Antonio Voyager had left any **TRACE** of his journey to Atlantis there. The Thea Sisters followed him inside.

The rooms on the first floor were mostly **EMPTY**.

"There doesn't seem to be anything interesting here," Violet remarked.

"Let's try going up!" Pam suggested, pointing to the staircase.

They marched up the **narrow** stairs in single file. The rooms on the second floor seemed to be just as empty as those on the first floor.

"I don't see any **clues**," Nicky said with a frown.

Everyone looked disappointed. They were about to leave when Violet suddenly let out a cry.

"Hey, look at the floor!"

Violet pointed to an almost invisible design at their feet. The floor of the room was made of stones. In the center of the room, the **stones** had been arranged in a circular pattern.

"It's the symbol of Atlantis!" Paulina realized.

It was the same symbol that appeared on

Atlas's **medallion**. To anyone else, it would look like a simple decoration. But they had recognized it, and Atlas was studying it carefully. He pointed to a rectangular stone in the center of the design and frowned. There was no **rectangle** in the symbol of Atlantis.

Nicky noticed his expression and knelt down to examine the stone.

"This **SLAB** is made of a different kind of stone," she remarked. She tapped on it with her paw, and a hollow sound echoed

through the room. She tried to lift up the stone, but she couldn't.

Pam knelt by her side. "You just need a little more **muscle**," she said. She easily removed the slab, revealing a small **HOLE** underneath it.

Nicky saw something glittering inside. "There's something here!" she exclaimed.

It was a small box made of a **SHIMMERING** red metal. Atlas picked it up and held it in his hands. Then he gave it to Paulina and pointed to his medallion.

"Do you mean that the case and the medallion are made of the same METAL?" Paulina asked.

"**Orichalcum**," Atlas said, carefully pronouncing the word.

"What did you say?" Pam asked.

"He said 'orichalcum,'" Violet repeated.

"It's a type of metal that is only found in **Atlantis**," Paulina explained. "This box must have come from there!"

Excited, she opened the box and found two pieces of **rolled-up** scroll. She unrolled the first and showed it to the others: It was a map.

"A **map**!" Violet cried. Then she frowned. "But look, the edges are ripped."

Colette gave it a closer look. "It seems to be a small piece of a larger map."

"Let's see what the other scroll is," Paulina said, **gently** unrolling it. It was a message, and she read it out loud.

"**It's him! It's Antonio Voyager!**" Nicky yelled when

I, Antonio Voyager, bold explorer of unknown worlds, present this account of my greatest voyage — a voyage to the depths of the sea.

There, I reached a secret kingdom where I saw things that no mouse on Earth has ever seen: Atlantis. I lived there happily for many years, but when I grew older, I wished to see the land of my birth one last time. The king allowed me to leave on one condition: that I never reveal all that I had seen.

However, I believe that a secret this wonderful is worth sharing, but only with those who are pure of heart. If you are reading this, you are a worthy explorer. You have found the first fragment of a map that will lead you to the underwater kingdom. I have hidden the other fragments in other cities I have visited. Remember: In water you will find the key.

Good luck,

Antonio Voyager

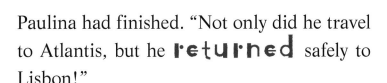
Paulina had finished. "Not only did he travel to Atlantis, but he **returned** safely to Lisbon!"

Atlas sensed that his friends had found something important. As he examined the map, a **happy** look came over his face.

"Voyager said that he hid the other **pieces** of the map," Paulina reflected. "We just need to figure out where he hid them."

"How will we **FIND** them?" Violet wondered. "We don't know where Voyager lived after he came back to Lisbon. His name isn't in any **history books**, remember?"

The Thea Sisters exchanged glances and answered the question at the same time.

"WE'LL ASK THEA FOR HELP!"

WAY TO GO, COLETTE!

Then they all became quiet; they heard **HEAVY STEPS** coming toward them. Suddenly, a rodent dressed in dark clothing burst into the room: **PROFESSOR QUASAR**!

The Thea Sisters gathered in front of Atlas, protecting him.

"**There you are!**" Quasar yelled. Then his voice became **sickly** sweet. "I've looked for you everywhere, my dear mouselings. Just go back to Mouseford, leave your friend here, and **MOVE ALONG.**"

"No way!" Paulina cried. "We know all about you, Mr. Beta!"

Quasar took a step forward, and Atlas stepped up to face him with **angry** eyes.

The **FAKE** smile on Quasar's face disappeared. "No more Mr. Nice Mouse," he said with a sneer. "This is serious business. You mouselings have no idea what trouble you're getting into."

"We're smarter than you think!" Pam shot back.

Quasar took another step closer. "**YOU CAN'T ESCAPE!**" he said menacingly.

Colette rummaged through the pockets of her jacket. "I have an **idea**," she whispered to her friends. "Leave it to me."

Then she put herself right under Quasar's

snout with her paws behind her back.

"What a pale complexion you have," she said, taking the professor by surprise. "You could really use some of . . . THIS!"

She waved her powder puff in his face, flooding his snout with white dust. Quasar began to sneeze and rub his eyes. He couldn't see!

"Hurry, run!" Colette yelled to the others.

They all ran past Quasar and raced back down the stairs. Colette was the last to leave, and before she did, she squirted Quasar right in the face with perfume.

"How about the smell of **Mousey Sighs** to top it off?" she asked.

STUNNED by the makeup assault, Quasar stumbled around the room, coughing and sneezing.

"Let me know when you're ready for your next **beauty treatment**!" Colette yelled as she fled down the stairs.

Quasar shook his paw angrily. "Don't fool yourselves . . . *cough!* I'll get you!" he called after her.

When the Thea Sisters and Atlas reached the street, they hailed a taxi.

"Hurry! We need to get out of here!" Nicky urged the driver.

Paulina immediately began to type on her MousePhone.

"Who are you calling?" Violet asked.

"We need help, fast," Paulina replied. "I'm writing to THEA!"

THE SILK ROAD

While the Thea Sisters were in Portugal, I had combed through the **dustiest** archives in the Mouseum of Rodent History. They contained **documents** collected from many unusual sources.

The collection was a mess, but I finally found a **manuscript** that told of the travels of a Portuguese explorer with the initials **A.V.** Could it be Antonio Voyager?

According to the story, a young EXPLORER had been asked by the king of Portugal

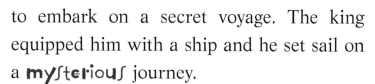

to embark on a secret voyage. The king equipped him with a ship and he set sail on a **mysterious** journey.

The ship never returned, and the explorer was thought to have been lost at sea. But twenty-five years later, he reappeared in Lisbon.

Whenever anyone asked him where he had been, he gave them a **bizarre** response. "I was in another world," he would say with a **mysterious** smile.

After he returned to Lisbon, A.V. became an ocean trader. He **traveled** to Constantinople and Africa, following a strip of the ancient SILK ROAD. This route united the Chinese empire with the West. Merchants followed the route over land, seas, and rivers to reach **China** and buy silk. Then they would return to Europe and sell it there.

I couldn't believe what I was reading. The details seemed to **MATCH** what Atlas had told us about Antonio Voyager. When I told the Thea Sisters what I had discovered, they decided to follow the Silk Road to see if they could find the **HIDDEN** map pieces. They took a *plane* to Istanbul, Turkey, the city that was formerly known as Constantinople—the first city that Voyager reached on the Silk Road.

"Thea has done it again," Colette remarked, looking at the **MAP** I had sent them.

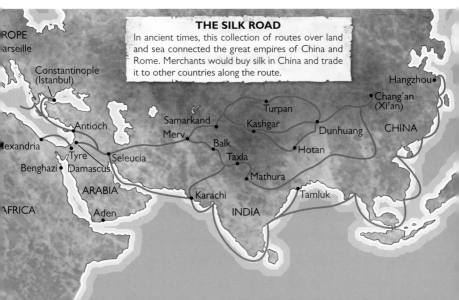

THE SILK ROAD
In ancient times, this collection of routes over land and sea connected the great empires of China and Rome. Merchants would buy silk in China and trade it to other countries along the route.

"Now we know where to **LOOK**," Paulina agreed.

Then her MousePhone beeped, and it was Kelly this time. Paulina answered it.

Hi Paulina — we have put together a gadget that will let you communicate with Atlas. Where should I send it?

To Istanbul, Turkey. Thanks!

When the plane landed, the Thea Sisters discussed their next **MOVE**.

"We don't have a specific place to search this time," Colette pointed out. "What should we do? **Search** the entire city?"

Just then, someone bumped into Colette. "Ex-excuse me," he muttered.

The clumsy rodent had a bushy **MUSTACHE**. He awkwardly bowed and tipped his hat to Colette. Inside the hat she could see the I.I.S. symbol: a **TOWER**.

She smiled, understanding, and the rodent winked at her. "Miss Colette, this is for you," he said, handing her a paper-wrapped package with an initial **K** in the corner. Before she could say thank you, the messenger DISAPPEARED.

The package contained six **BRACELETS** and a card that read, "Each of you put on a **BLUE** bracelet, and give the **GReeN** one to Atlas."

"Look!" Colette cried. "This must be the communication system that Kelly invented."

She was right! They each put on a bracelet. When Atlas began to speak in his melodious language, each one of them understood him perfectly.

"Where have you brought me?" he asked.

DISCOVERING ISTANBUL

Finally, Atlas and the Thea Sisters could speak **NORMALLY** to one another!

The mouselings immediately began to explain why they were in Istanbul.

"The other scroll we found in the tower was a letter from Antonio Voyager," Paulina told him. "He said he **HID** the other pieces of the map in cities he visited."

"Thea discovered that he traveled to Constantinople and Africa, following an old **TRADING** route," Colette went on. "We know that he was here in **Istanbul**, but we don't know where to look!"

Atlas looked at the **fragment** of the map,

and then he asked them to read the letter to him.

"Those words at the end were **interesting**," he said. "Can you read them again?"

"'In water you will find the key,'" Violet repeated.

Atlas nodded thoughtfully. "I feel that those words are an important **clue**."

"Istanbul is surrounded by **WATER**," Nicky remarked. "There are so many places we could start looking."

Paulina opened up her guidebook. "Let's start in the **middle**!" she suggested.

They all took a taxi to the center of the *busy* city. They began to walk around and soon came to a building with

a sign above the door that said HAMMAM.

"A *hammam*!" Colette cried happily. "It's a Turkish steam bath!"

"Did you say 'steam'?" Atlas asked. "Does that mean there is water there?"

Colette nodded. "Usually, the rooms have **fountains** of steaming water that you use for your bath. Maybe we should check it out!" She got a dreamy look in her eyes.

"This building didn't **exist** yet during

Voyager's time," Violet pointed out. "I don't think it's useful for us to go inside."

"Let's keep moving!" Nicky suggested.

They walked across the Galata Bridge, crossing over the Golden Horn, a **CANAL** that divides the city into two parts. The majestic **GALATA TOWER** stood on one side of the canal, offering a fantastic view of the beautiful old **buildings** in the city.

Atlas looked discouraged. The city was so big!

"Don't worry," Paulina reassured him. "We'll find the **MAP**!"

They left the canal behind them and began to explore the crowded streets of old buildings. They kept their eyes open, looking for anything that might be a **clue**.

Then Atlas stopped suddenly in front of one of the buildings. "This . . . this is **orichalcum**!" he cried with wonder.

A small plate of SHIMMERING

red metal was attached to the stone wall. Nicky got a closer look and saw the number 3.36 engraved in it.

"Check out this number!" she said.

"What is this place?" asked Pam.

Violet consulted the guidebook. "It's the **Sunken Palace Cistern**, an old underground storage tank for water. It was built in the sixth century CE by the Romans."

"Did you say water? Maybe this is the **WATER** we're looking for," Pam guessed.

They entered and walked down several flights of stairs. The air grew moister with each step. They finally ended up in a large, dimly lit space. It was eerily quiet, and rows and rows of **TALL COLUMNS** held up the arched ceiling. Water covered the floor, and the only way to explore was to walk along one of the narrow footbridges.

"Maybe the number on the sign means something," Violet WHISPERED, looking around.

"There are three hundred thirty-six **COLUMNS**," Paulina said, reading through the guidebook. "That's three-three-six."

"But a dot separates the numbers on the sign," Atlas pointed out. "In his diary, Antonio Voyager used this notation to give coordinates. He might mean three degrees north and thirty-six degrees west."

"That's possible," agreed Nicky. "Or the numbers could refer to the **ROWS OF COLUMNS**. You know, the third column in the thirty-sixth row."

"Or the thirty-sixth column in the third row," Paulina added.

"Let's check it out!" Pam cried.

She went with Nicky and Colette to check out the third row. Atlas, Paulina, and Violet headed for the thirty-sixth row. Soon Paulina's voice rang out.

"There's something here!"

At the base of the column, there was a stone carved with the symbol of Atlantis!

"We found the clue!" Violet cried, and she ran to get the others.

Atlas **removed** the stone from the column, revealing a small hole behind it. Inside was a small orichalcum **BOX**, identical to the one they had found in Belém Tower. Atlas was beginning to open it when he and Paulina heard a familiar voice behind them.

"YOU CAN'T ESCAPE ME NOW!"

HOW DOES QUASAR DO IT?

A **plump** rodent popped out from behind the nearest column.

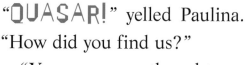

"QUASAR!" yelled Paulina. "How did you find us?"

"You mean you thought you got rid of me?" he asked with a **WICKED** sneer. "Ha! Now you're coming with me," he said, moving toward Atlas.

Paulina **JUMPED** in front of the prince.

"Give it up, mouseling," Quasar said with a laugh. "You can't **STOP** me this time!"

Before Paulina could prevent him, Quasar lassoed her with a **rope**, pinning her arms to her body. She couldn't move! She tried to

Wiggle free, but the rope only seemed to get tighter.

Quasar laughed. "Fight all you want, but it won't do you any good. This rope is a special **invention** of mine. The more you pull on the knot, the **TIGHTER** it becomes!" he bragged.

Atlas whispered in her ear. "Don't worry, I will free you. Trust me."

He turned to the professor, and with a daring look on his face, he LEAPED off the footbridge into the water!

"Where are you going?" Quasar said angrily, as Atlas disappeared under the water. "Are you just going to leave your friend here? **What a cowardly thing to do!**"

He leaned over the rail, shaking his paw. But what he didn't realize was that Atlas had

swum *under* the bridge and was now on the opposite side. The prince took off the sash that he wore around his waist and tied one end to the railing of the footbridge. Then he threw the other end to the other side and tied it, so the sash stretched **tightly** across the path behind Quasar's back. Quietly, he snuck up behind the professor.

"Here I am!" Atlas cried in his musical language.

Quasar could only hear a song behind him. Confused, he turned around and suddenly saw Atlas.

"I'll get you!" he cried, running forward. But he didn't see the sash, and tripped right over it! He fell into the water.

Nicky, Violet, Colette, and Pam came running up just in time to see Quasar fall.

"**GOOD JOB!**" Nicky told Atlas, who was already *untying* Paulina.

Atlas tucked the orichalcum box into his tunic. "Let's go!"

They **QUICKLY** ran up the stairs and emerged onto the street. They didn't stop until they reached a park.

"Atlas, thank you," Paulina said. "If it weren't for you . . ."

"I am happy to help you. You have done so much for me already," the prince replied with a smile.

He took out the red metal **BOX** and opened the lid. The Thea Sisters gathered around to see what was inside: another piece of the **map**! The top edge matched perfectly with the piece they found in Lisbon.

"We've got it!" Pam exclaimed.

"There's still **one piece** missing," Nicky said, gently tracing the outline of the map with her paw.

"I'm **sure** we can find it," Paulina said confidently. "That is, as long as Quasar doesn't find us again."

"By the way, how does he keep **finding us**?" Violet wondered. "It's as if he always knows exactly where we are. First Argentina, then Portugal, and now here!"

At that moment Colette's **pink** MousePhone rang. "It's Thea!" she cried. "Hello?"

"Hi, Colette!" I said. "I finished reading that manuscript about **VOYAGER**. After Istanbul he went to Africa—to Ethiopia, where he stopped at a place called Tis Issat."

"That must be where the **third piece** of the map is!" Colette said, excited. "We'll go there right away."

She hung up the phone, and noticed Paulina looking at her thoughtfully. "Coco, can you give me your PHone for a second? I need to **check** something."

Colette gave it to her friend, who opened it up and took out the **battery**. Paulina peeled off a small dark metal plate and showed it to the others. "Just as I thought! There's a **transmitter** in this MousePhone!"

"A what?" Colette asked.

"This is the **PHONE** you got from Ruby's party, right?" Paulina asked, and Colette nodded. "Remember when **QUASAR'S** assistant gave you back your purse? That's when he must have put the transmitter in the phone. It's a chip that allows Quasar to **locate us**. That's how he's always able to find us!"

"WE NEED TO THROW IT OUT IMMEDIATELY!" Nicky cried.

Pam grinned. "Don't do that. I have a better idea . . ."

TRICKED!

Professor Quasar stopped to mop his forehead, which was drenched with **sweat**.

"Those mouselings," he muttered. "Leave it to them to travel all the way to the **SAHARA DESERT**!"

Around him, the **SAND** dunes of the desert extended as far as he could see.

"I've already been following their **signal** for two hours," he complained.

He hoisted his backpack on his back. It held all the supplies he needed to set a proper **trap** for the Thea Sisters.

"This time they won't be able to escape," he mumbled. Then he headed up the next sand dune, grunting and **groaning** as he climbed. He gazed down at his transmitter, and the **R E D L I G H T** began to blink quickly. He was close.

"I've got them!" he exclaimed.

He climbed down the dune and saw a small oasis in front of him. Among the palm trees were some Arabian camels SLOWLY walking toward a small pool of blue water.

Confused, Quasar looked at his blinking transmitter. The Thea Sisters should be here, but there was no sign of them! How was that possible? The device that his assistant had hidden in Colette's MousePhone was very sophisticated. It never lied.

One of the camels noticed Quasar and approached him, sniffing him curiously.

"Shoo!" the professor exclaimed crossly, waving his paws at the camel.

The animal didn't listen to Quasar. It CHOMPED down on Quasar's hat, pulling

it off of his head.

"Stop! That's mine!" Quasar yelled. He yanked at the hat, but **stopped** when he noticed something odd. The camel was wearing a strange collar.

"What is this?" he asked, examining the collar. Then he erupted in **RAGE**. Someone had placed the TRANSMITTER from Colette's phone around the camel's neck!

"Nooo! I've been tricked!" he howled.

Without his device he had no way of knowing where the unpredictable mouselings were headed. Had he failed?

Maybe . . . **but maybe not**. He knew that there was one place where he would find them again, sooner or later.

SOME UNEXPECTED HELP

The Thea Sisters and Atlas were calmly seated on an airplane headed to Ethiopia.

"I wonder where Quasar is now?" Nicky asked, chuckling. "I would love to see his expression when he finds the transmitter in the middle of the SAHARA DESERT!"

"It's a good thing we lost him. Now we can focus on our next destination," Violet said seriously, taking a guidebook to Ethiopia from her backpack. She read out loud. "'*Tis Issat* is the ancient name of the Blue Nile Falls. It means "smoking water." You can get there by bus from Bahir Dar.'"

"We're about to LAND in Bahir Dar!" Nicky said happily. "I'm glad Thea organized

this trip for us. Now all we have to do is look for **CLUES** to the third map."

"I think we need to look for a place that is truly *special*," Violet commented.

"What do you mean?" Atlas asked.

"So far, this adventure has led us to three extraordinary places," she replied. "The

WATERFALLS of the Iguazú River, the tower of Belém, and the **cistern** of Istanbul. Who knows what awaits us in Ethiopia?"

Atlas smiled. "Yes, there really are some **extraordinary** places in this world."

Once the plane landed, they made their

way to the **BUS** that would take them to the **BLUE NILE FALLS**. Once they boarded the bus, Violet read aloud.

"The guidebook says that the falls are **SPECTACULAR**. I'm sure Voyager must have left the third piece of the **map** somewhere nearby."

The bus quickly arrived at the falls. It *was* a spectacular sight. **Lush** green trees surrounded the falls, which **CASCADED** down a rocky ridge. They followed the guidebook's directions to a path that led to a flat area overlooking the waterfall.

"Wow!" Nicky exclaimed.

"It's beautiful," Paulina said, "but I don't see any **clues** here, just a lot of plants."

"Let's **explore**," Nicky suggested.

They walked down a muddy path to the riverbank.

"Now what?" Colette asked, frowning at the **mud** on her pants.

"Now we look for the symbol of Atlantis!" Nicky said.

They slowly walked along the water's edge. Suddenly, Colette let out a terrible scream.

"Aaaaaaaaaaaaaah!"

"What's the matter? Did you fall in the mud?" Pam teased, without turning around.

"A CRO . . . CRO . . . CROCO . . ."

"A crock of soup? I'm **HUNGRY**!" Pam joked, looking back. She gasped. An **ENORMOUSE** crocodile was right behind Colette!

The friends were paralyzed by **FEAR**.

"Stay calm . . ." Colette whispered.

"Let's back up **VERY SLOWLY**," Pam said softly. But just then, a **young** rodent with a stick popped out from the bushes.

"Shoo!" he yelled at the crocodile. He spun the STICK, frightening the creature. "Get out of here! Go!"

The crocodile **SLID** back into the water as the others raced up to them.

"We owe you our thanks!" Pam told the young mouse, **smiling**. "My name is Pam. These are my friends Colette, Nicky, Violet, Paulina, and Atlas."

"**MY NAME IS DABIR,**" he replied, eyeing them. "What brings you to Ethiopia?"

"We're **exploring** the falls," Violet explained. "We're looking for—"

Dabir wasn't listening. His attention had been captured by Atlas's **MEDALLION**.

"I've seen that **SYMBOL** before!" he said, reaching to gently touch it.

The Thea Sisters were **STUNNED**!

THE FINISHED MAP

"The symbol is carved into an ancient **rock**," Dabir told the Thea Sisters. "It's not too far from here."

"Can you please take us to see it?" Paulina asked him. Everyone was thinking the same thing: Was this the final **clue**?

Dabir agreed, and he asked them to climb into a **small** rowboat with him. He steered them down the river, then stopped by a clearing that contained abandoned **ruins**.

When they got off the boat, Dabir pointed to one of the crumbling ancient columns.

"See?" he asked, pointing to the **symbol of Atlantis** carved into the stone. The mouselings exchanged excited glances.

This had to be it! Atlas began to scan the

surface of the rock with his hands, searching for where the third piece of the map might be **hidden**. But he didn't find anything.

"This time it seems more difficult than before," Violet mused. "Grandfather Chen always says, 'If you don't find an answer, take a minute to sit and **meditate**.'"

She sat down on a rock right next to the column, and immediately heard a *loud*

CLUnK!

The column rumbled and then began to **ROTATE** on its base, until two stones in the side of the column lined up and one of them slid open. Inside they could see the gleaming red metal of a third orichalcum **BOX**.

"Fantastic!" Pam cried, hugging Dabir. "Thank you for taking us here!"

The young mouse saw how **happy** his

new friends were, and he smiled.

Atlas impatiently opened the box and gave the last piece of the **map** to Paulina, who pieced it together with the first two fragments.

Violet gasped. "But that's incredible!" she exclaimed. "It's **WHALE ISLAND**!"

Dabir looked at the map. "What is it?"

"That's the island where we live," Colette explained, still dazed. "So after coming all this way, we need to go back to where we started?"

"It makes sense," Violet realized. "After all, Atlas washed ashore on the beach of Whale Island. One of the **BLUE CURRENTS** must pass by there."

"Dabir, could you take us **BACK**?" asked Pam urgently. "We need to get to the airport!"

"Of course!" he responded. "But if you have time, I would like to show you my **home**."

The Thea Sisters and Atlas all looked at one another, doubtful. They were **eager** to return to Whale Island. But Pam's stomach decided for them when it let out a loud growl.

Dabir smiled. "My house isn't far from here. You can **taste** some of my mother's delicious food. Then I will take you right to where the bus stops without us having to **climb** back up from the river."

"That sounds great," the THEA SISTERS agreed, and they followed Dabir to his hut. A delicious **SCENT** floated from inside. When they entered, Dabir's mother offered them a plate of large **Flatbread**.

"It's called *injera*," Dabir explained. "You hold it in your paws and use it to scoop up the rice, vegetables, and **sauce** on the plate so you can eat them all in one bite!"

Everyone loved the delicious dish; it was just what they needed before the start of another long journey. After thanking Dabir and his mother, they returned to the airport and took the first *FLIGHT* back to Whale Island.

THE RETURN TO
WHALE ISLAND

Vince Guymouse's hydroplane rode the BLUE waves surrounding Whale Island as it took the Thea Sisters home.

On the trip back from Africa, Paulina had called Kelly and told her everything they had DISCOVERED. Then Kelly had told the Thea Sisters about the decision to keep Atlas a secret.

"At the I.I.S. we will study all of the information that everyone has collected," she explained. "But we still need to do more *research* before we make it public. We need to protect the citizens of Atlantis from rodents like Mr. Beta."

When they docked at the port, Ruby Flashyfur was there, waiting for her closest friends, Alicia, Connie, and Zoe, to return from vacation. She had been alone at the deserted school for days. Everyone seemed to have VANISHED!

As she watched the passengers leave the hydroplane, she was SURPRISED to see that the Thea Sisters had returned, along with the fascinating blue-skinned boy. They seemed exhausted, as if they were coming back from a **LONG** and tiring trip.

Ruby was irritated. *Those boring mouselings went out with the mysterious stranger and didn't invite me!* she thought.

"Hi, Ruby!" Nicky called out cheerfully as she and the Thea Sisters walked down the dock. But Ruby just turned her snout in the air and looked away.

"I see nothing much has changed here at Mouseford," Violet remarked.

Right at that moment, Ruby received a **MESSAGE** from her friends.

We missed the hydro-plane! Alicia got lost in the Forever Furry store in the new mall. We'll come back tomorrow. Don't be mad!

Connie, Zoe, and Alicia

"**GRRRRR**," Ruby fumed. Her friends were never on time.

The Thea Sisters had already left the dock when a small **BLACK HYDROPLANE** pulled up.

Ruby **recognized** it. "Professor Quasar!" she called out.

She **RUSHED** to the craft and began bombarding him with questions.

"Did you start **FILMING** your documentary yet? You said I could have the lead part in it, right? Is it okay if I wear a green silk dress, to go with the ocean?"

Quasar ignored her chatter until he heard her say, "And don't let the THEA SISTERS and their strange friend be part of the film. Just now they didn't even say hello!"

Quasar's whiskers twitched. "JUST NOW?" he asked. "You mean, they're here?"

"Yes, I just saw them go into town," Ruby replied. "You know, I think—"

But she didn't **FINISH** her sentence. Quasar was already scurrying away!

The Thea Sisters, meanwhile, had met up with **Kelly**,

who landed on the ISLAND in an I.I.S. helicopter.

"We need to take a boat out to meet the Blue Current," she said, after studying **Antonio Voyager's** map. "Then Atlas can use the current to get home."

"Let's ask **LEOPOLD WHALE**," Pam suggested. "He already knows **Atlas**, and we know we can trust him."

reminder of me. And who knows . . . maybe one day we'll **see each other** again!"

Leopold's voice rang out. "We're here!"

Then Atlas and Paulina's Quiet moment was interrupted by the **ROAR** of a motor.

"OH, NO! It's Mr. Beta!" Kelly yelled. The **WICKED** scientist was driving a

reminder of me. And who knows . . . maybe one day we'll **see each other** again!"

Leopold's voice rang out. "We're here!"

Then Atlas and Paulina's Quiet moment was interrupted by the **ROAR** of a motor. "OH, NO! It's Mr. Beta!" Kelly yelled. The **WICKED** scientist was driving a

QUASAR'S LAST CHANCE

Paulina stood at the rail of the ship, her long braid dancing in the WIND. The sea was beautiful, but her **heart** was filled with **SADNESS**.

Atlas approached her. "I always believed that the **BIGGEST** adventure of my life would be out in the world above the surface," he said. "But after meeting you all, I realize that the best adventure is keeping good **friendships** with you always."

Paulina smiled, trying to hold back tears.

"Before I leave, I want to give you a gift," he said softly. Then he took off his **medallion**.

"Your medallion?" she asked in shock.

He smiled. "I want you to keep it as a

who landed on the ISLAND in an I.I.S. helicopter.

"We need to take a boat out to meet the Blue Current," she said, after studying **Antonio Voyager's** map. "Then Atlas can use the current to get home."

"Let's ask **LEOPOLD WHALE**," Pam suggested. "He already knows Atlas, and we know we can trust him."

Leopold was happy to provide his **fishing boat**, and Atlas asked him to bring along a smaller longboat as well. He needed to take the last leg of the trip **alone**.

"Getting too close to the Blue Current could be **DANGEROUS**," he explained to Paulina. "I'm not sure what will happen and I don't want to put any of you at risk."

Before they left, Leopold studied the **map** and figured out where they needed to go. Then the fishermouse got behind the wheel and the boat chugged away from shore.

The sky was **BLUE**, the sea was calm, and everything seemed to be going smoothly. But the Thea Sisters didn't know that someone dangerous was **following** them. . . .

hydroplane loaded with all kinds of strange **gadgets**. When he neared the fishing boat he aimed a harpoon at it. The hook LATCHED on to the boat's deck.

"Now you can't get away!" Quasar cried.

He held up a metal globe with rods sticking out of it. "Thanks to this sleep-wave transmitter, you're all about to take a nice little nap! **HA HA HA!!!**"

He lifted up the transmitter and got ready to toss it onto the boat. Once everyone was asleep, he planned to **KIDNAP** Atlas.

Before he could throw it, two **dolphins** bobbed out of the water. Atlas called out to them in his **musical** language. The dolphins seemed to understand him and immediately zoomed toward the hydroplane. As they **BUMPED** into it with their snouts, the craft swayed dangerously.

Quasar **wobbled** back and forth, and the sleep transmitter slipped out of his hands and fell into the water. Then he lost his balance and **fell** overboard, tumbling into the waves.

SPLASH!

The dolphins joyously jumped through the water, **PUSHING** the professor back and forth with their snouts. He cried out in protest, but they HAPPILY ignored him.

Pam gave Atlas a high five. "Nice!"

"But since when do you **speak to dolphins**?" Paulina asked in amazement.

Atlas grinned.

"As long as I can remember," he replied. "The Atlantean language is the same as theirs. It's also the same language that **WHALES** use."

"Aha!" Nicky exclaimed. "Then it's not just a coincidence that a **BLUE CURRENT** passes by Whale Island."

While they talked, Leopold scooped Quasar out of the water with a net. Then he trapped him inside a pile of **LIFE PRESERVERS**.

"This is the strangest fish I've ever caught!" he said with a laugh.

GOOD-BYE, ATLAS

Finally, Atlas was ready to leave. He had the **map** to use to find his way home.

"Will you be able to find the **BLUE CURRENTS**?" Violet asked him.

"It will be tricky, but they will help me," he said, pointing to the dolphins Swimming in the waves.

Atlas hugged each of the Thea Sisters and climbed aboard the longboat.

"Thank you from my heart, my friends. Good-bye!"

The Thea Sisters watched him as his boat slowly disappeared from view. Paulina wiped a tear from her eye.

"Don't be sad," Kelly whispered to her, putting a **PAW** on Paulina's shoulder. "I've got

a feeling it's not really good-bye."

Atlas's boat was now just a speck on the horizon. "Something tells me that we'll see him again," Kelly said. "There is so much left to discover about his extraordinary world. I am convinced that this is just our first contact with it."

After the boat had completely disappeared, they headed back to shore. Ruby Flashyfur was waiting IMPATIENTLY on the dock. When she saw the Thea Sisters with Professor Quasar trapped inside the life preservers, her eyes grew wide.

"What are you thinking?" she yelled. "Don't you know that the professor is FAMOUSE?"

Kelly anchored the boat, shaking her head. "I'm sorry to

disappoint you, but this rodent is actually a **fraud** and a thief. I would strongly advise you to stay away from him!"

Ruby turned pale. "A . . . a fraud? But he promised to make _me famouse!" she stammered. Then she stomped off, confused, angry, and disappointed.

As Ruby left, Headmaster **OCTAVIUS DE MOUSUS** walked toward them.

"Good morning, Thea Sisters!" he called out. "Ready to start classes?"

When Kelly saw him, her face **lit up**. "How wonderful to see you, Professor!"

The professor grinned and hugged her. "Kelly Parker! It's been a long time, but I remember you well! You and Thea Stilton were such promising students. I'm sure you've become a great **scientist**."

"Indeed I have," Kelly replied, "and I owe

it to your wonderful lectures."

The Thea Sisters and Leopold were so interested in watching the **happy** reunion that they didn't notice that Professor Quasar was slipping out of the life preservers.

When they were done talking, they realized Quasar was *GONE*.

"**OH, NO!** He escaped!" Pam cried.

Kelly shook her head. "That rodent is very clever," she said. "But at least we stopped him from carrying out his **SUSPICIOUS PLANS**."

The Thea Sisters agreed: Their adventure had come to a close.

A GiFT FROM FAR AWAY

School was back in session, and the Thea Sisters returned to their usual routine, knowing that their **FRIENDSHIP** was stronger than ever. They would never forget their incredible encounter with Atlas, and already treasured the memory in their hearts.

One day, Mercury Whale, the island's mailmouse, found a strange **package** on the beach. It was wrapped in a SHIMMERING golden fabric. The label looked like a piece of blue algae and there was no address, just a drawing of the THEA SISTERS. Luckily, Mercury knew them and brought the package to Mouseford Academy. As soon as they saw it, the mouselings knew who it was from: Atlas!

The package contained five GOLD tiaras, each one topped by a large pearl. In a separate box there was a large shell.

Violet studied the shape of the shell. "It could be a musical instrument," she mused.

Each mouselet put on a tiara and they all walked down to the beach. Paulina, who was wearing Atlas's medallion, blew into the shell. sweet music filled the air.

"It almost sounds like Atlas's voice," Colette said dreamily. "Do you think he's trying to tell us something?"

"The bracelets!" Paulina remembered, and they

put on the translation bracelets that Kelly had given them.

Paulina blew into the shell again. This time, they clearly heard Atlas's voice.

Dear friends, I have finally returned to my kingdom! I am so happy to be home again, but I will never forget you. I sense that we will see each other again one day!

The Thea Sisters looked at each other and smiled. Now they knew that the **power of friendship** was strong enough to reach between worlds. What they didn't know was that at the sound of the **SHELL**, a school of dolphins gathered near the coast — ready to lead whoever made the **call** back to the Blue Currents!

Be sure to check out these exciting Thea Sisters adventures!

Thea Stilton and the Dragon's Code

Thea Stilton and the Mountain of Fire

Thea Stilton and the Ghost of the Shipwreck

Thea Stilton and the Secret City

Thea Stilton and the Mystery in Paris

Thea Stilton and the Cherry Blossom Adventure

Thea Stilton and the Star Castaways

Thea Stilton: Big Trouble in the Big Apple

Thea Stilton and the Ice Treasure

Thea Stilton and the Secret of the Old Castle

Thea Stilton and the Blue Scarab Hunt

Thea Stilton and the Prince's Emerald

Don't miss these very special editions!

THE KINGDOM OF FANTASY

THE QUEST FOR PARADISE:
THE RETURN TO THE KINGDOM OF FANTASY

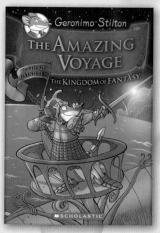

THE AMAZING VOYAGE:
THE THIRD ADVENTURE IN THE KINGDOM OF FANTASY

THE DRAGON PROPHECY:
THE FOURTH ADVENTURE IN THE KINGDOM OF FANTASY

Be sure to read these stories, too!

#1 Lost Treasure of the Emerald Eye

#2 The Curse of the Cheese Pyramid

#3 Cat and Mouse in a Haunted House

#4 I'm Too Fond of My Fur!

#5 Four Mice Deep in the Jungle

#6 Paws Off, Cheddarface!

#7 Red Pizzas for a Blue Count

#8 Attack of the Bandit Cats

#9 A Fabumouse Vacation for Geronimo

#10 All Because of a Cup of Coffee

#11 It's Halloween, You 'Fraidy Mouse!

#12 Merry Christmas, Geronimo!

#13 The Phantom of the Subway

#14 The Temple of the Ruby of Fire

#15 The Mona Mousa Code

#16 A Cheese-Colored Camper

#17 Watch Your Whiskers, Stilton!

#18 Shipwreck on the Pirate Islands

#19 My Name Is Stilton, Geronimo Stilton   **#20 Surf's Up, Geronimo!**   **#21 The Wild, Wild West**   **#22 The Secret of Cacklefur Castle**   **A Christmas Tale**

#23 Valentine's Day Disaster   **#24 Field Trip to Niagara Falls**   **#25 The Search for Sunken Treasure**   **#26 The Mummy with No Name**   **#27 The Christmas Toy Factory**

#28 Wedding Crasher   **#29 Down and Out Down Under**   **#30 The Mouse Island Marathon**   **#31 The Mysterious Cheese Thief**   **Christmas Catastrophe**

#32 Valley of the Giant Skeletons   **#33 Geronimo and the Gold Medal Mystery**   **#34 Geronimo Stilton, Secret Agent**   **#35 A Very Merry Christmas**   **#36 Geronimo's Valentine**

#37 The Race Across America

#38 A Fabumouse School Adventure

#39 Singing Sensation

#40 The Karate Mouse

#41 Mighty Mount Kilimanjaro

#42 The Peculiar Pumpkin Thief

#43 I'm Not a Supermouse!

#44 The Giant Diamond Robbery

#45 Save the White Whale!

#46 The Haunted Castle

#47 Run for the Hills, Geronimo!

#48 The Mystery in Venice

#49 The Way of the Samurai

#50 This Hotel Is Haunted!

And coming soon!

#51 The Enormouse Pearl Heist

Meet
CREEPELLA VON CACKLEFUR

I, *Geronimo Stilton*, have a lot of mouse friends, but none as **spooky** as my friend CREEPELLA VON CACKLEFUR! She is an enchanting and MYSTERIOUS mouse with a pet bat named **Bitewing**. YIKES! I'm a real 'fraidy mouse, but even I think CREEPELLA and her family are AWFULLY fascinating. I can't wait for you to read all about CREEPELLA in these fa-mouse-ly funny and **spectacularly spooky** tales!

#1 THE THIRTEEN GHOSTS

#2 MEET ME IN HORRORWOOD

#3 GHOST PIRATE TREASURE

#4 RETURN OF THE VAMPIRE